WOLF SONG

ALEX H. SINGH

DEDICATION

You are all music notes in my life. Ones that have created a beautiful melody. This novel "Wolf Song" is to all of you.

ALSO BY ALEX H. SINGH

FALLEN KINGDOMS CHRONICLES

LAMP OF LIGHT

-

SECOND CHANCES NOVELLAS

DESIRING DEMURE

LIGHT & DARK

-

NUBARA

DESTINY AWAITS

ORIGINS OF THE RISEN

-

FAYETED

OBSCURA

GRAPHIC

THE SECOND HUSBAND

MOONLIGHT ECSTASY

RITE TO REIGN ANTHOLOGY

PROLOGUE

he ground around the large hall was wet from the rain. The once blue sky had turned dark giving way to short moments of clarity through the lightning that was often followed by wailing crescendos of thunder. The rain had been falling for over an hour and a half but it seemed not to have disrupted the large hall to be filled to the brim even before the main recital. The Manhattan hall was built more like the ancient Roman coliseums with largely rounded pillars bearing the different figures of gargoyles.

Even though lights were shining so bright from every corner of the hall, the stage shone brighter with a variety of colors to indicate the special attraction effect to captivate the audience. It was regarded as the largest and most well-planned orchestra ever as it was strategically organized when people from all over the world would be on holiday and would be around without worrying about the stress of work or the tension of having to wake up early to go to school.

"T-minus 20," a tiny voice which one could have misconstrued as that of a lady said to Melody.

It was the voice that had ushered her to where she was presently. While it was not that friendly before, it had turned to be more jovial at every heads up it was giving. At first, she thought it was his words that sent a chill down her spine, but as she stood up when the man was no longer there, she was still shivering.

What she felt was not just stage fright, but something more— the human nature. She had long lived hidden among humans to know them. Having the ability to read emotions and the myriad of moods humans experience clearer and more accurately than the ordinary man might seem like a good idea at first, but it was not helping her in most ways. In her experience of being part human and part wolf, she had seen the hypercritical ways in which humans deal. How quickly they jump to conclusions and most especially how easy they criticize and pass judgment on others.

That night, her amplified hearing ability was hearing lots of comments from the crowd. Her hearing caught all sorts of random things, ranging from the kids asking when they will leave the hall, to the ones asking where they will visit next as they were tired of the orchestra. She was not just hearing the kids but the older people were not beyond her hearing and it was what they were saying that made her have second thoughts in performing that night. Bored husbands were eating snacks voraciously to avert any discussion form their wives and the single males were making funny jokes about the orchestra members to score a point or two with the ladies that might end up in their bed that night.

Humans can't see art. They are just so blind to the beauty that exists all around them, she thought to herself.

She shut her eyes tight to block out the world around her. What she wanted most was to stay fully connected to her human self, as it was the only way to block out numerous voices that were distracting her from the task at hand. At first, it worked but it didn't last for more than a few seconds as the wolf part of her gradually took over all her senses.

She sighed and began her breathing exercises with a deep inhalation followed by a calm and gentle breath out. She moved towards the path leading to the stage for performers. Although she was a professional, a musical prodigy and she had won many awards after performing on hundreds of different stages in different countries, she always felt as if it was her first performance before she hit the stage. Upon reaching the curtain that blocked the light emanating from the hall to shine on her face, she grasped her instrument before she removed the veil. Melody walked slowly to the seat prepared for her beside her fellow performers who were also waiting for the time the pre-show music resounding through the hall to be over. She tried her best not to look at the audience as she felt it might affect the confidence she was short of at the moment. But the curiosity to see with her eyes overpowered her.

At first, she was blinded by the light, the hypersensitivity of her eyes hurt her more than most due to her shifter side. She had learned to respond to stimuli in a normal way by imitating the way humans will respond, so as not to be tagged as being weird.

Gradually, her sight was gaining back its function as it first processed the numerous heads staring toward the direction that she was seated. Almost at the same time, the time for her to perform came. Flawlessly and without showing much effort, she placed her violin on her shoulder. She closed her eyes for few seconds but opened them faster than she closed them. String by string, with every drag and push, she drew all the attention of the audience to the sounds she was producing. Above the song, she could feel the calmness and less noise and distraction as she played.

It was about fifteen minutes that she had been playing and the audience was not merely paying rapt attention to the music, they were acting as if under a spell as the music drew them into its charm like a siren's song. Tears began to form in the eyes of those in attendance and others were trying hard not to go too emotional by the harmonious way the song was coming out.

The music was not just enchanting to the audience but also to Melody, as she closed her eyes to absorb the emotions and the present state of everybody. However, as she shut her eyes, the absence of the stage lights caused these gruesome images to begin playing like a film reel behind her eyelids.

BLOOD WAS ALL AROUND, TWO BODIES WERE LYING LIFELESS ON THE floor. Just as she was about to look at who they were, she opened her eyes. When the lighting of the hall hit her, the intensity of the music increased. She poured her emotions out through the music, even though she knew it would no longer be enough to contain it. These dark thoughts made tears begin to stream out of her eyes drop by drop.

The most stone-hearted members of the audience at that moment were fully encapsulated under the spell of her music now as tears shone on everyone's faces. She kept playing not minding the downside of exposing people to such a sad atmosphere during their holiday time. All the time she was playing she was concentrated on a single location which was her fingers upon her instrument. She made them slide gently on the bow while she carried on with what she was playing.

After about thirty minutes of spectacular music, she looked up towards the audience one more time before she slowly stopped the music. It took everyone that listened to her some moments to come back to reality but when they did, they all gave a standing ovation. The parents who carried babies or had lots on their laps found ways to allow their legs to raise them for the ovation. She took a bow as she was known to do when she noticed an outstanding person also on his feet.

He was about six feet tall with a slim body that made him seem like a young guy in his prime but his pale wrinkled body would testify against that. His Irish look was striking even with the effect time had on his handsomeness.

They both stole a glance at one another and she gave another mild bow to him just before the maestro joined her side. He bade everyone to hold their adulation as he had something to say. They were not compliant to this but when they noticed that the maestro just stood on the spot looking and smiling at them without saying anything they began to sit one after the other.

"Give it up for this young angel with the strings," he complimented as he made a gesture for the audience to express their appreciation.

They replied with enthusiasm as they began to shout and scream with joy and satisfaction. Melody was not feeling too good as this was going on but she thought it was because of the crowd and the noise that was overwhelming her so she tried to suppress them all.

The maestro began to tell the crowd who she was. She was the niece of a legend; Donovan Prescott who also possessed the ability to arouse emotions, break the heart and mend souls with his music before he died from heart complications.

"But he didn't just leave us like that," he shouted to the crowd, "He managed to give us a worthy protégé in the form of his beloved niece," he said pointing at Melody.

This made the whole crowd shout again as they now chanted her name. The maestro put his hands on her shoulders as he tried to hold back the thought of her uncle's demise and the struggle the young girl had to pass navigate the often dog eat dog world that is the music industry alone without a parent or guardian while growing up.

But unlike the maestro, the introduction gave Melody the feeling that she had been able to carry on with the name of her uncle and the standard he had laid down before his death. She smiled as she felt proud of this feat but then, the feeling she was having before came roaring back.

"I am done with the performance," she thought, trying to decipher why she was still feeling a bit out of sorts and quite unlike her normal self.

Her mind was still processing this when the ground began to feel as if it was moving. She raised up her eyes to see if it would be better, but it wasn't. The people around her were also moving in a random motion. Then it dawned on her.

"I am feeling dizzy,"

She tried to compose herself with all the strength she could muster but the more she tried, the more she failed. With the last vestiges of her remaining strength, she staggered to the back slightly, then to the front and without much thought, she stumbled to the front, this time faster. The maestro saw what was happening so he motioned to catch her just when she was about to reach the floor. The whole audience gasped in surprise and confusion as to what was happening to the star of the night who looked healthy and well until her dramatic collapse.

"Are you alright?" the maestro asked her patting her cheek to keep her eyes open.

She looked at him with her eyes half-closed but it was all blurry to her. She was lifted from the ground to her feet by him and didn't leave her till she looked capable of standing on her own. They both turned to the crowd to see their reaction to what just happened.

"You are alright Melody?" The maestro uttered to her making his words sound like a motivation than a partial question.

Melody was feeling better again as she opened her eyes wide. But she knew that she was not going to be like that for long so she turned to leave the stage. She could feel the emotions of all that was around her and this made her brain buzz with the emotional maelstrom. She took a step towards the edge of the stage when suddenly her eyes rolled back in her head and her consciousness began slipping away. Again, she made her way to the floor with her head leading the way speedily, her eyes closed waiting for the pain to come in case she didn't go unconscious before hitting the floor. In a jiffy, the pain rushed through her veins starting from those in her head which forcibly struck the stage floor.

When this was happening, the maestro was farther away from her which made his move to catch her again futile. All he had were empty hands hanging in the air. Once it was clear that it was too late to catch her, he knelt by her side not sure of the precise thing to do to revive her.

From the agitated and confused crowd who were not clear on the next line of action for them, a man came rushing forward just in time to knee beside the maestro. He received a skeptical gaze from the maestro kneeling next to her as he was neither an official nor a colleague that the maestro knew of. Upon deciphering the look, he explained himself before he touched her.

"I am a doctor," he stated "Please clear the space for me to examine her," he ordered looking at the maestro knowing he was the only one who could get all the crew that had blocked the air around her away.

Immediately, he moved his hands to instruct the crew members to clear out. The doctor checked her pulse and gave a sigh of relief having discovered that she was still breathing, although quite faintly. He helped readjust her gown back to its full length so she would not feel exposed in front of so many shocked audience members, peradventure she opened her eyes.

With all that just happened, she was already looking pale like someone who had been struggling with a disease for years. Her naturally pink lips now resembled the color of a withering red rose. Even, her hair which seemed lustrous and sparkling, flowing while she was performing now seemed lifeless and dried out.

By this time there were only a few people remaining on the stage and her eyelids were struggling to flutter open, the maestro was touched from behind. Without turning he knew who it could be.

"The ambulance is here," the voice said sotto voce.

On cue, the uniformed paramedics came in with equipment while some of them moved the stretcher to the stage to carry the unconscious virtuoso. As she was carefully placed on the stretcher and carted away, the maestro followed them. he had taken few steps before he stopped suddenly remembering something.

"Alfred," he called on the senior conductor who rushed towards him to hear what he had for him.

"You are in charge now."

He also turned to the doctor that rushed to revive her.

"Thank you." he passed along his thanks.

"It's my job," the man replied.

The maestro gave a weak smile before disappearing to the backstage exit. The outside was very cold from the relentless rain and the crowd of onlookers stood still on seeing the ambulance to know what exactly was wrong. The engine of the ambulance was still on in preparation to take off once the patient was loaded in. When this happened, the maestro could not get to the door of the ambulance fast enough before it zoomed off. As if he knew it was going to happen, his silver 2014 Audi wheeled to where the ambulance was once parked. A much younger man came out of it with a security uniform.

"Spot on Jake," he commented.

He entered the car and sped off into the street of Manhattan following the light emanating from the ambulance.

It had been over forty minutes now that the maestro had been in the waiting room. During this period, he had paced the hospital from one hallway to another looking through the transparent walls of some ward. When he could no longer stand the waiting, he gravitated to the corridor where the doctor attending to Melody passed with the hope of seeing him.

He had barely taken two steps when the doctor came out from a ward. The doctor managed to smile at him but the maestro knew better than to believe the authenticity of the smile. He shook the doctor's hand before rapid-firing all the questions he had at him.

"She is awake now," the doctor stated first to him before responding to any of the other questions.

He allowed the maestro to give a sigh of relief before he uttered the next word and during this period, he tried to search through his mental dictionary to look for a less unpleasant way to deliver the news he had. It was the hardest part of the job description, it was written all over him.

"The patient," he started.

"Melody," the maestro corrected him.

"Melody has cancer," he gave out in a single breath.

The countenance of the maestro changed from bad to worse upon hearing the diagnosis but the doctor knew it would be better to give the details of what kind of cancer so that he could go through the pain all at once.

"The cancer is a particularly virulent form of lymphoma and it's currently at stage two,"

The doctor pointed the direction of his office to him so they could talk further, away from any ear that might be listening to them but it was too late. Melody had already heard all that she needed to and it all came as quite a shock to her. *Cancer*.

Her mind drifted back to the time when she was very young and was first diagnosed with it. She could remember the tears and negative emotions that befell her family upon receiving the diagnosis and how they made a vow to do whatever they could in discovering a treatment plan to heal her.

Tears began to form in her eyes when her thoughts went to the sacrifice that was made to get her healed by her parents but she held it back. She felt warm... just like the time her mother touched her years ago during her first transformation. She smiled at her before she was ripped to shred in the most inhumane way ever. Knowing that she could no longer compose herself, she slid back on the bed with tears in her eyes.

"All that for nothing," she thought to herself.

She noticed someone moving towards her and she had to fake sleep so the person would pass by her without asking any questions or showing pity. When the person was no longer close she opened her eyes and as if she was in a trance, she found herself staring at herself; but a younger version. It was when she was 4 years old when she was still fighting the cancer.

She looked fragile and without strength from the rapid rate at which the cancer was attacking her body. Her parents were also there at the park with her that day and even though she could not remember the precise time of what she was staring at that happened in the past, but she knew it was real.

Her parents were smiling at her as they watched her play around with other kids and their pets. She didn't stay long here as she was all of a sudden yanked to another location. It was dark outside and she was alone. The only source of light was the full moon that could be seen through the window. The moon was shining brightly in the sky that night.

Her parents had promised that they would be back for her soon, and that there was nothing to fear in the woods as long as they are close by. While she knew it might not be the truth, there was little she could do as a four-year-old kid who had no one but her parents. Melody tried to talk to her parents but they were not aware of her presence as she was just in her own memory.

After about ten minutes into her parents' departure, she knew what happened next but stood to see it one more time. It was the day that changed everything for her and her family. Off in the distance a twig snapped, not long it was followed by another then the sound came closer and quicker towards her. There, without warning, a mighty wolf jumped out of the woods into the house, breaking the door down.

Its body was hairy. The fur covering its body was a pure white color with no spot whatsoever. Its teeth were out and saliva was dripping from its muzzle as it moved closer to her. Beneath the hideous look that it had, its reddish grey eyes were very gentle and with compassion. It was as if that made her not scream.

As she could not be seen, she moved closer to the wolf to catch a glimpse of it again before it attacked her younger self. Even though she had seen it too many times to count its elegant body never ceased to amaze her. With agile swiftness, it jumped on the younger Melody and gave her series of bite marks. Unlike the nature of wolves after attacking, the wolf neither ate her nor was it seen leaving her. Instead, it disappeared without a trace.

The wetness of the pillow on the bed was what dragged her back to the present world. She knew the cancer was not just affecting her, but it was also causing damage to the creature inside her; the main reason she had survived this long without having a single day of illness or any health complication.

"I am dying," she murmured testing the words out in the silence of her hospital room.

"We are dying," she gasped in fear upon realization.

This thought kept her up all night and only one question kept resounding over and over in her mind.

"How am I going to save myself? How am I going to save the last majestic white wolf? How do I prevent the extinction of the royal wolf?"

1

———————

The sun had a very funny way of showing reflection around the hospital. This was not the only thing Melody had been subjected to. She had also been subjected to being greeted by the different nurses who all had a sad undertone to the smile they gave her.

It had been three days since she found out her most dreaded fear had returned to her. Every minute she spent in the hospital bed revealed different things for the nurses treating her. They found out in her file that she once had cancer when she was young and it went away miraculously.

"What a poor girl," one of the nurses commented.

Melody's ears were filled with lots of stories about what could have caused her cancer to come back, and why did it have to reoccur just when she was about to reach the pinnacle for her career. Not only this, they made speculations about what could have cured her in the first place. At that moment, she no longer cared about her health in the hospital, all she wanted was to be away from the gossip that only added to her pain.

Her special ability to hear clearer and better than any ordinary human was meant to be a gift from the majestic white wolf. It was now proving to be a curse as she could hear everything being said about her and it was causing her to feel sicker than she ought to with cancer.

When the noise finally died down she finally laid her head on the pillow that had become her only companion since she got to the hospital. Just when her eyelids started to droop closed and were almost entirely shut, a voice came again and it seemed to be from the drug store.

"You heard about the patient with cancer?" One of the nurses asked another.

"The musician? Melody?" he inquired.

"Yes,"

"Who wouldn't? I heard her name was actually Sophia Nestor but it was changed when she started staying with her late maestro uncle not long after her parents were attacked by an unknown vicious beast out in the woods.

"It is really a shame that her life is going on this way," the first nurse commented.

"Real shame, I tell you. Lots of death surrounding her already," the other said.

It had been years since someone ever referred to her as Sophia and it was a big surprise for her that someone knew that much about her. The name took her mind back to the time when she was young. She remembered the very day that changed it all. It was during recess, she was playing with her friends, they were jumping over the bouncer when she started to feel dizzy and suddenly blood was gushing out of her nose. She was rushed to the school health center but when the nurse in charge saw the treatment she was giving might not be enough for her, she called her parents to come down to the school. The school nurse advised them to take her to the hospital for a proper checkup as they lack proper equipment in the school's health center.

The day of their appointment with the doctor came faster than she would have thought. She was looking thin and in poor health already. Her parents were the first to hear the news; the result of the myriad of tests that were carried out on their daughter. When they walked out of the doctor's office, she could tell even at her tender age the sadness that the news had on them. Mixed feelings set in when she asked what was exactly wrong, they didn't tell her at first- not until they were out of the hospital and back in their home.

She remembered the journey from the hospital to her house because her mother, whose face was always wearing a smile that made her dimple stand out, was devoid of a smile. Even her father, David who was supposed to be the pillar of strength holding the family together in times of trouble, was saddened by the news that Sophia had yet to know about. Innocently, she had asked what was wrong with them and what the conversation that her parents had with the doctor was about. Instead of responding to her question, they simply sighed and looked out the window.

It got to a time when they were caught in the traffic; her father looked back and kissed her forehead.

"I love you my beautiful Sophia. Your mom and I, we really love you and will do anything for you." he uttered.

Although his intention was to comfort her, he only scared her more. No doubt, her father was a very loving and caring man. He was not the type that always expressed his emotions in the way that he just did and this sent fear trailing down her spine.

"Tell me what's wrong Dad?" she demanded her voice sounding authoritative despite her diminutive size.

She had been told by her peers in school that she had a strong character. The reason for this was not far-fetched. Her scholastic side was well nurtured by her father who had a military background. Although he now worked in the engineering profession, he could have been easily mistaken for a military man. This bearing was reflected in the way he carried himself and even raised his child. His daughter had unconsciously took after him in this aspect.

When she knew that her father would not be moved by her question, she turned to her mother.

"Mom, what are you guys hiding from me?" she demanded from her this time her tiny voice expressed anger and frustration.

"It is my body, remember?" she spoke again.

The light had already turned green before anyone could reply to her. David had been thinking of many ways to get her to stop talking so when he saw the green light came on, he stomped on the gas and took off with increased speed. He wanted nothing more than to get home quickly. Her mother didn't say anything but Sophia could hear her sob.

"I hate doctors, they always say bad things," she commented angrily.

After another ten minutes' drive, her father parked in front of their house. It was a bungalow-style that looked as if it was just repainted. Her father was known for his perfectionist nature which made him notch some time out of his busy schedule to paint the house himself any time the color was looking in the least bit faded.

He was quick to exit the car and without waiting for his wife or daughter he entered the house and retired to his bedroom. To avoid being questioned by Sophia again, her mother had sent her straight off to her room to do her assignments. But having noticed the harsh way she dismissed her, her mother; brought her favorite fruit drink and lots of chocolate to appease her.

Sophia took the opportunity to ask her what really happened in the hospital. She gave her mother the pitiful but cute eyes that she always used on her to avert scolding and it seemed to be working this time to get the information she so desperately wanted to know from her.

Candace sighed as she held her daughter close to her bosom.

"You know life is not just a fairy tale, sometimes it can be so unfair," she started to talk.

But before she could utter more words to what she had already said, the door to Sophia's room creaked open and her father suddenly appeared in the doorway. One moment, he was looking fine although sad, but as he looked down to see them it was as if he was running a temperature. It was the first time Sophia had seen him since they got back from the hospital. She would have liked to give him a hug but he only took a long look at her mother then a short one at her before leaving the room shaking his head.

"Stay in your room, I will be right back," her mother said, kissing her forehead before exiting her room to follow her husband out.

The house was ghost quiet. The only thing Sophia heard were the birds of the night calling and the crickets' sounds, which were clear that night until it changed. Voices began to be heard, it was first coming like a loud conversation to Sophia but slowly it dawned on her that her parents were having a very loud argument. They were both screaming at the top of their lungs. She crept out of her room to see what on earth could have been the matter. It was the first time that she could remember hearing her parents talk that loud at each other or even have a misunderstanding.

"She's too young to understand what's going on," her father screamed at her mother.

"It's her body. You can't just hide such a thing from her," Candace fired back.

"We should be the one protecting her. Let's wait until we have a solution or a treatment plan then we can tell her. Telling her now will destroy her just like it is destroying us," David explained to Candace.

Having seen that all the drama was about her, she moved out of the corner that she was hiding in. Her father was the first to see her.

"What are you doing out here dear?" he asked with an entirely different voice and tone that he used seconds ago. The voice was filled with pain and love at the same time.

"Go to your room sweet pea. Dad and I are talking about boring grownup stuff." her mother added with a smile

Sophia looked at them for few seconds, thinking of what the right thing for her to do was. Although she didn't know exactly what they were shouting about, she did know their fight was all about her and something the doctor said. By the way things were going, her mother wanted to tell her, her father was of a different opinion.

"No," Sophia objected with a low voice.

"What did you say dear?" her father inquired from her to be sure that he heard her right.

"I am the cause of this, and I want to know what is wrong. I am scared." She said as she burst into tears now.

The duo moved together towards her. Her father picked her up and placed her on his lap while her mother wiped the tears from her eyes. David sighed then he began to speak.

"There is something your mother and I want to tell you," he stated.

Candace looked surprised at her daughter. Minutes ago, David had been stiff-necked to the fact that the state of Sophia's health had to be kept a secret but now he planned on telling her.

Sophia left his lap to sit opposite her father and her mother joined her side. Her father first off assured her that they were going to do all that was in their power to find a cure. When he was sure that her mind was prepared to hear it, he told her that she had cancer.

All she could do was look at them with a teensy-weensy bit of sadness. While she had heard lots of things about cancer, she was yet to know the intensity and implication that comes with living with it. Her mother started crying and this made her heart heavy too. She began to shed tears on her mother's lap, this made David move closer to them as he wrapped his arms around both of them. He drew the two of them into his broad chest and the entire family let their sadness flow out and around them.

She started going to the hospital for checkups and experimental treatment regimens frequently while her parents were also looking for a cure. One Thursday morning, after over a year since her diagnosis, her father came home with rather pleasant news. He looked very happy about his new discovery and it reflected on him.

When asked about what he had discovered by his wife, he explained to her what his secretary told her of a man named Ishtar who was a powerful Shaman. He told them he was known to cure diseases that modern medicine has yet to find their way around and his new secretary was very sure that he could cure her.

That night, there was happiness in the house. The new found solution was viewed with cautious optimism. After over a year since the discovery of her cancer, the house had been a cold, dead environment with no joy and happiness. The only time they made time to talk was when they stopped to discuss Sophia's health. Although they did their best as parents to make her psychologically okay, they sometimes fell short of this when they saw her pale and thin body. Her hair was already falling out and this added to her parents panic, especially her mother.

They all planned to visit the much talked about Shaman at Echo Cove, a small town that was not too far from New Jersey the very next day. Which made them all head to bed early with the hope of a cure and a better tomorrow in mind.

It was Candace that woke up first. Without waiting for others, she started preparing the meal they would takefor breakfast and also some sandwiches for lunch just in case they were late coming home. David woke up not much later to help with other things while his wife attended to their daughter.

They left home before the sun in the sky could get the chance to show its full power through its piercing rays. David was not one to drive very fast especially when their daughter was onboard but it was different that day. He complained at every red light and mumbled angrily at any driver that made him decelerate.

After spending a few hours driving, they got to Echo Cove. The town was indeed small. The only thing that pointed them in the right direction was a billboard that had been covered with shrubs hanging all over it.

"We are here," David announced to them, turning the wheel towards a gravel road.

The town was more of a village with little glimpses of civilization showing around it. The car had just traveled for few minutes before they came in contact with small houses closely packed together. As they drove past, people kept looking at them in a rather unusual way and it gave the impression that they were not used to seeing visitors around their town.

David having realized this parked his car close to a nearby bush so as to ask directions to the shaman from anybody closest to them.

"Stay in the car, please ladies," he instructed them.

"Be careful," his wife warned him.

He looked back to see if she meant it as a joke but seeing her eyes, he knew she was not actually joking about it.

"I will," he replied.

He took a glance at Sophia sitting in the backseat and smiled.

"You will be alright dear," he consoled before leaving the car.

He walked to the road, in which he just moved his car away from to see the closest and the less threatening person he could walk up to, but to his surprise, the people he could see were all looking tense and it gave the sensation that they were all in mourning.

Having observed everyone, he made up his mind to inquire about the directions from an old man who was smoking tobacco out on his porch early that morning.

"Hello there," he greeted.

The man was leaning on the railing and with not a care in the world of what to do with his old age. Judging from the side view in which David was looking at him, he looked like a man in his early eighties, his head had wisps of white hair scantily distributed on his head. Not only was his back bent towards the railings that supported him but it looked like his back was positioned the natural way. His bad posture must have been caused by heavy loads or perhaps an injury in his younger days.

"Top of the morning to you laddie," the man turned to greet him, it was as if David's words ignited something in him. The man who seemed like a lifeless old man moments ago greeted him with much vigor in his words.

Even though he was old, his teeth were sparkling clean and his lips were very pink like that of a kid. It gave the impression that he was neither an alcoholic nor a smoker even though David had just spotted him with tobacco. Having exchanged pleasantries, he inquired where he might locate the shaman and it was then that the old man's eyes turned cold again.

"What do you want from that crazy old fool?" he snapped, his voice filled with hatred and distrust for him.

Not minding the things the old man had to say about the shaman, he reiterated his need to locate the man. When the man saw that David was not going to take no for an answer, he pointed the way to him.

At first, he thought he was pointing him in a wrong direction. All David could see was a small path leading to the woods. But just when he was about to turn back to confirm if that truly was the correct direction, he saw a tiny well-worn footpath which gave the impression that people do pass through that place often.

He thanked the old man for his help and headed hurriedly to the car. He quickly relayed the direction to his wife as he carried his daughter on his shoulders out of the car. They walked into the woods to see where the road will lead them.

The woods were calm that morning with flapping wings audible to them. It was like walking in a well-cultivated forest as each tree stood clear from one another. They got to the end of the pathway as it was barricaded by a large rock and on the rock sat a man with his back to them. Even though he must have heard them approach, he did not move an inch from where he sat.

They stood still for a while to see if he would turn towards them but as minutes went by it seemed implausible. Candace greeted him aloud impatiently but still, he neither moved nor made a sound.

"I think he is deep in the spirit," Sophia said in her father's ear.

"Yes, you are correct," the voice suddenly came startling them.

It was a rough and loud voice that carried lots of charisma. David and Sophia were surprised that he could hear what she said because Candace who was closer could not have heard them. They greeted one another and Ishtar the shaman offered them a seat on the rock.

"Do you want a drink?" he asked them.

The three of them looked at one another and as if communicating with their eyes, they reached a disaffirming conclusion. Ishtar was a very young man, younger than any of them would have thought. Even though he looked as if he had never stepped foot into any institution for formal education, the way he carried himself was enviable. His face was fresh. It was without a beard or even so much as a mustache, his hair was neatly packed beneath the transparent head warmer he had on and this made him look even younger.

After explaining the reason they came to him, he first declined to help them claiming that the risk involved was much too high and the sacrifice they would have to pay is much more than they would want. The duo was not ready to give up on the only chance their daughter had of surviving, so they begged him vehemently. Then, he gave them a simple instruction.

"On the day when the moon will shine brightest, leave the flower in the woods," he uttered a cryptic parable.

While Sophia didn't know what he meant, her parents knew exactly was he was saying. After the day in which she was left in the woods, her parents rushed inside the cabin where they kept her for the night and didn't find her and instead, a trail of blood was all they could follow. Following it to the end, they found their daughter with bite marks on the side of her ribs and she laid unconscious on the floor as she had lost so much blood.

Visibly shook up, they rushed her to the hospital telling the medical personnel that they were attacked by an unknown beast the previous night when they went camping. To everyone's surprise, she healed from the wounds much faster than they thought and when the day for her weekly checkup came, the doctor was shocked as he noticed that the cancer was no longer present. He ran the blood test over and over again but it still yielded the same result. When he delivered this news to the family, they were very ecstatic and thankful to the shaman who had helped them. Three weeks of joy came to the family after months of unspeakable sadness and silent tears but the night for another full moon soon arrived. Came.

A noise woke Candace up that night and when she went out of the room to see what was happening. She discovered that the noise was the sound of glass breaking and it was coming from their daughter's room. By the time she started heading to her room slowly, David had already joined her, carrying a baseball bat that he got from the hall closet. When they were in front of her room, they could see the pieces of the broken door on the ground and this made Candace gasp in fear of what might have happened.

"Stay back," David told her shoving her behind him as he moved forward towards the room.

When he faced the already ajar door, he stood still. This made his wife worried because she was oblivious to what had made her husband stop in fear. A very big wolf with white fur and the only stain on it was on its paws which were covered with blood. On seeing them, the wolf moved forward slowly, showing its teeth in a threatening way and in an instant, he rushed towards them. As David was the closest to the door, it got to him first. He was swiftly bitten on the neck which made him bleed out instantly from a punctured carotid without much struggle. The only sound that came out of his death was the sound created by the blood that was gushing out of his broken neck.

Candace screamed in fear as she rushed to the sitting room and hid behind the sofa. While this had shielded her from the beast for some time, it didn't take long for the angry beast to sniff her out. The wolf turned to where she was hiding. Their eyes met. She rushed to her daughter's bedroom to see what was left of her. While running, she did her best not to look at her dead husband. She was sure that would cause her to breakdown and that was not what she needed at the time. All she had in mind was to get to her daughter if she was still alive and run for help. On getting to the room, she didn't see Sophia or her body. Instead she saw her pajamas, the ones she got for her as Christmas gift the year before covered in blood.

The wolf must have given up on her as it had yet to get to the room. She saw traces of blood, the tiny footprint of blood on the floor that led to the bathroom, she also saw the print from her daughter's palms also in blood at the entrance of the bathroom. This made her rush inside thinking it was where the wolf finished her off but on getting there, it was just the demolished bathroom that she saw. The bulb illuminating the bathroom was now blinking lowly. With the poor illumination, she saw the blood mark she was trailing. She had to strain her eyes to see the print clearly but she noticed it was different from the one she followed inside.

The footprint had been replaced by a different one— paw prints. On seeing it, her mind went straight to the words of the shaman who warned them of the sacrifice they would have to pay. Tears began to flow from her eyes as she went out of the bathroom. It began to dawn on her, the wolf didn't kill her daughter; the wolf was her daughter.

Her legs became weak from running and from the shock of her discovery, when the wolf finally sniffed out her location. The burning fury in the wolf's eyes shone distinctively in the room. Candace knelt down knowing what was going to be her fate. The wolf moved slowly like it did the first time when it attacked David. It kept looking at Candace like it was not sure of what she was doing. In fear, she screamed out loud which made the wolf change its pace to a much faster one towards her. She whispered softly with a smile as the large teeth clamped down into her neck.

"Momma loves you baby girl," she said closing her eyes gently as life left flowing from her body with every breath that she took.

It was during this time that her uncle Donovan became her legal guardian being the only adult available to take her in. She was not close to her uncle for a very long time as the trauma of losing her parents was still much in her. She was not the only one to blame for this distance though as her uncle was not always home for any form of heartfelt conversation.

It was one of the days when he wasn't around and her babysitter was not early that she heard a piece of classical music playing loudly from a neighbor's open window. She felt some sort of peace settle inside her and the beast in her was also as calm as she was. She made her uncle get all the classical music he was able to think of for her, even though he didn't know the truth about why she wanted them. After much practicing, she was able to find a unity with her two sides. Her communication with the wolf was always telepathically. The music drifted her to an astral journey to a very large oak tree. In this trancelike stare, only two entities existed— her and the Majestic White Wolf.

She was about to fall deeper into the memories of her past again when she felt a touch on her body. Her concentration had been fixed from what she was thinking about that she didn't smell the heavy stench left by drugs and disinfectant on the doctor. When he tapped her, she felt alarmed and disorientated.

The doctor discharged her and gave all the medical advice that he could think of. Melody did nothing but stare at him knowing that none of his prescriptions would work for her. She knew what she must do no matter how sad or fearful it seemed.

"I must go back to Echo Cove. I must beg the shaman to free the wolf from me. It cannot die with me. I must go back," her subconscious voice uttered slowly to her.

2

The sky was very clear. The sun had cloaked its' elegance behind one of the white fluffy clouds giving it all its rays to disperse it to other clouds. Melody had walked into the music academic hall about half an hour ago to ask for the maestro but was told he was in a meeting. She knew with her special wolf skills that he had been sitting inside his office since she arrived soliloquizing on what he could say to convince her not to make the decision she was about to take. But it was too late, her mind was already made up.

When she was discharged, she had made calls to professionals that would get her condo sold fast and she had also withdrew all the inheritance she had in just ten days of being discharged. Maestro, without being told, knew what she was doing. She wanted to spend the time left alone, wallowing in the pain and agony of her life but he didn't want that for her but he also knew he had little say on her decision.

When her stay at the receptionist's office was getting awkward, she decided to walk around and probably see her colleagues to give her final goodbyes. She told the receptionist she was leaving, knowing that they could draw the maestro out when he was sure she was no longer in the vicinity.

She went to the practice room but stood by the door to hear the music that her companions were rehearsing. It was one of her favorites and she hummed it silently as they played. But the music stopped halfway through the piece and that surprised her, she could hear footsteps coming closer to the door but before she could move away, Jason opened the door.

"Hey you," he said in his usual jovial manner.

Jason was one of the most controversial friends that Melody had. He was the one that heightened her love for violin as against the keyboard that she started with. After a sleepless night and long hours of practice, he was able to make her keep up to the standard needed.

"Hey there," she replied with a smile.

Jason hugged her tightly and he subtly dragged her inside the room. Upon seeing her everybody dropped their respective musical instrument to greet her.

"We thought you wouldn't ever come in," one of her companions jested.

"What do you mean?" She asked skeptically.

She looked in the direction of the door to check if she could see what he meant and it dawned on her that she had been a fool all along. The door had been changed to a translucent glass, everyone inside could clearly see who or what was outside while the person outside would be completely unaware of this.

She gave a gentle smile at this. It was the first real smile that ever came to her lips since the incident in Manhattan Hall. She had wanted to leave but was begged to play even if it were to be her last performance for them. She gave in to this and picked up the closest violin. Without backup or anything, she played the violin part of the song they played for the soldiers' memorial that had the President in attendance a year before.

The music calmed all of them and the sound carried to the maestro who had finally came out of his office thinking he had frustrated her plan to leave. As he opened the door to see who the person playing the violin was, he was surprised to see that it was Melody- the person he had thought to have left the hall. Their eyes met and gradually, she reduced the sound of the music till it faded into nothing. She was applauded as she dropped the violin where she picked it up from.

"Promise you will call me when you get to wherever you are going?" Jason asked.

But instead of replying or giving her words, she hugged him and pecked his cheek.

"Maestro," she called as she saw him walking slowly in the hallway.

He turned towards her but she could see the sadness reflected in his eyes and his eyes had turned red from tears. Aside from the fact that he was her teacher, he was like a guardian to her especially after her uncle died. They spoke about different things as they walked to his office but as he opened the door for her, she stood still. She explained why she needed to leave him leaving all the essential details out so as not to create another question in his mind. He dragged her close to himself as he wrapped his arms around her.

They stayed like this for a few minutes not minding that they were standing by the door. When they later let go of each other, tears were flowing uncontrollably from her eyes. They said their goodbyes as she left for the bus stop to catch a bus going to her destination.

Being a place that was seldom visited and filled with people who still held on to the old ways, buses going to Echo Cove were not easy to find. She had to wait until evening for the next bus heading that direction to come as she had missed the afternoon bus she planned on catching. During the time she spent waiting, she reprocessed her mission once again. It was the only thing she had to do before cancer got the better of her.

"I am going to stay close to Echo Cove and search for Ishtar." She mumbled to herself.

"He did this, he should be able to know what would reverse this. He has to," she spoke to herself again but this time it was louder.

"Excuse me?" the man carrying a suitcase asked beside her.

"What is that?" she asked the man calmly although she didn't like the idea of her thoughts being interrupted by someone she didn't know.

"I thought you were referring to me," he stated looking lost. "You mumbled some things and I thought you were talking to me," he said.

Melody shook her head to inform him that she was not talking to him. She assumed her former position again but as she was still trying to find out where she left off in her thoughts, the bus they had all been waiting for came.

Eagerly, they walked on board the bus. With the look of the passengers that they met inside the bus, they were coming from a far place and already tired of just sitting on the bus. She quickly used her eyes to scout for a perfect place for her to sit where she would not be disturbed. She didn't have to search for long when her eyes caught an empty seat at the far back of the bus. It was getting really dark and this didn't give a good view through the window.

Quickly, she moved to the seat but instead of placing her bags inside the cabinet designated for this, she put it beside her to prevent anybody from sitting in the seat next to her. She didn't want to be disturbed and she was ready to go to any lengths to make that possible.

She was pleased with what she did as she had barely sat when the man who interrupted her thoughts at the bus stop walked to where she was, thinking the seat beside her was free. On getting there, he saw that her bags had occupied the other seat, he looked at her and gave a soft grin at the way she blocked the chance of anyone speaking with her.

The bus waited for another five minutes to make sure that everyone was already sitting comfortably before it zoomed off. When they were fully on the road and the bus was moving smoothly, she took out her phone and put on a very large headset to drown herself in the songs on her playlist.

It was about thirty minutes now that she had been on the bus. She took off the headset to see what was going on with other passengers. The man who had wanted to sit with her was already in deep slumber with his mouth half opened, she looked at him piteously before taking her gaze straight to other passengers. She discovered that most of them were also fast asleep while some of them had their ears plugged.

The civilization she saw out the bus window made her think she was ever going to see such sight again in Echo Cove. She slid back in her seat, putting her headset back on when the song that was on was getting to an end. It switched to a favorite song of hers- the Sound of Silence which she would commonly play to drift her to the oak tree where she could communicate with her other half.

As her mind took the journey, her breathing became slower. Like a flash of light she moved and was standing right in front of the oak tree. The oak tree since she became merged with the white wolf as a werewolf had remained the same, tall, with branches that cannot be easily reached and the floor was rid of any withering leaves or dirt whatsoever.

Having noticed her presence, the wolf appeared from behind the oak tree. It was looking as big and beautiful as ever and its eyes showed compassion. It knew what she had been going through. She not only shared the abilities of the wolf, the wolf also has a share in anything that happened to her. When she's sad, it will also be sad, if it was the other way round; the same will be for the wolf.

It walked slowly to meet Melody who was trying her best to give just as bright of a smile as she used to since they came together, but she was a bad actress. They walked to the oak tree where the tired looking Melody rest her back on the tree while the wolf went to the side it appeared from as it stood there like a sentinel, guarding her from any form of attack.

Most times that they see each other, they did not need to talk to each other to know what they had in mind but that day, Melody wanted to talk to it. So she took a deep breath and the cold mist could be seen passing out of her mouth and nose.

"I am dying," she started talking by first stating the obvious, the wolf gave a sad growl at this and she continued with her words.

"And I cannot bring you down with me," she informed the wolf.

"So I am going to find a way to make sure you don't have to go through this with me."

On hearing this, the wolf moved closer to her. It faced her with the saddest expression that Melody had ever seen on it.

"That is the only way, to get you out of my body. You have done lots of good things for me, it is time I return the favor," she explained the reason for her action.

The wolf, although it could hear her clearly but it looked very confused as to what she wanted to do. It moved very close to her and when it was close enough, it placed one of its paws on her chest.

"I know you will always be a part of me. But this must be done, you need to live on, you are the last of your kind, I am not." She uttered before breaking down in tears. She bent her head as tears fell irrepressibly down her cheeks and down onto her hands. She realized that as her tears fell on her hands, it was leaving splotches of red behind— it was blood. She was crying drops of blood. Scared of the rate at which she was depreciating, she pulled herself out of the trance with a loud depressing voice.

She looked around to see if anyone saw her reaction but it seemed they were unmoved by whatever she did. Not wanting to sleep again, she stopped the music, stood up and moved towards the only person she knew would still be awake-- the driver.

The driver looked at her quizzically not sure why she left her seat. His first thought was that she wanted to make an inquiry on when they will get to their destination. But the question didn't come. He replied promptly anyways without caring that she didn't ask him. With that Melody deduced that he was not much of a talker, so she sat in the nearest vacant seat to the driver.

When they had moved about half a kilometer towards their destination, the driver saw a deer up ahead, he honked at it in hopes that it will get it off the road, but it didn't budge an inch from where it was. This made him park to chase it off. Melody noticed that it was quite weird for a deer to stand like that with the feeling of contentment just to die on the road.

"They might be dumb animals, but they are certainly wise in averting death," she thought to herself.

She had wanted to object to the idea of the driver leaving the bus to chase it away but she didn't. Despite how much she wanted to, there would not be a way for them to pass. And aside from that, if she managed to tell him that she sensed danger, he would probably laugh her off.

With keen eyes, she looked around from inside the bus to see if she could catch a glimpse of what could be the real danger. While she didn't see anything, she felt the presence of another creature. A kind that was not created to be gentle. She sensed that it was filled with killer instinct and massive savage tendencies. Her thoughts arrived to a conclusion and she realized immediately what the animal was.

Instantly, adrenaline started pumping huge amount of blood all over her body, she started honking at the driver who was still outside. She signaled to him to come inside quickly. From the distance, she heard a tree branch crack and it was loud enough for him to hear it too. By the time he concentrated on the reason he was outside, the deer was gone.

They heard the cracking sound again but this time, it sounded closer then another followed. Melody knew there was nothing she could do to save him now, the predator had marked him. She turned to see the other passengers, some of them were just waking from their slumber having noticed that the bus had stopped. Taking the moment, she walked to the back of the bus, near where she sat. All of the passengers were now wide awake to see the gruesome scene outside by that time.

Feeling okay that nobody was looking, she sneaked out of the bus from the back, doing her best not to close it fully for when she would be coming back.

She bent her torso with her hands on her knees. Her back became broad and protruded. Then steadily her hands turned to paws while her straight legs curved till it became a hind leg, her face was also turning hideous with it taking longer than normal and her teeth becoming larger. Her four feet were on the ground now as she had fully transformed to a full-blown white wolf.

Wasting no time, she walked slowly to the front of the bus, waiting for the appropriate time to launch a counter-attack. A brown wolf had already pushed the driver to the ground but instead of attacking him straight up, it kept stalling. The driver was sitting on the ground and the cold that night was not enough to stop him from sweating.

Melody wanted to attack upon seeing it, but she knew wolves are always in a pack and it wouldn't be wise for her to charge without having full comprehension of what laid ahead. As if her mind was read, two wolves joined the brown wolf and they moved around the driver. Melody could hear the passengers panic and the little kids inside being objected from looking even though they wanted to.

The brown wolf that first wiped the driver off his feet bent to the ground to give a full lunge at the man, but just as it was at midair, the majestic white wolf came out, running towards the wolf with an exceptional show of force, it used the force of the brown wolf against him by lunging against him, the white wolf pushed the brown wolf to a tree by the roadside with force.

The wolf growled in pain and couldn't stand immediately from the pain that it had sustained, this made the other two prepare to charge against the white wolf, but when they saw that it stood its ground even though it knew it was outnumbered. They felt scared and ran into the bush instead. The white wolf gave a very loud howl looking up ahead at the full moon above.

When the wounded wolf recovered, it noticed that the other wolves were no longer there but it was not ready to give up the fight-not after it was humiliated in front of those that seemed like its subordinates.

It shook the dust off its body before moving towards the white wolf who stood guard in front of the driver and ready to attack from any angle. The driver took the cue to creep cautiously to the door of the bus. When he was safely inside, the wolves made threatening sounds to each other but having seen no way of winning the fight, the brown wolf ran into the bush taking the path chosen by its companions.

The white wolf waited for all to be calm before it went back through the path it came from. When it was sure of being out of sight, the white wolf swiftly morphed to Melody without breaking a sweat. She opened the back door and quietly entered. She sat on her seat with her ears plugged so as not to look suspicious. The bus driver, who after he had confirmed if everybody was okay moved the bus away with an increased speed.

When they were finally out of the place, Melody thought of the possible repercussions of what she just did. She knew she had just made enemies for herself.

"But I see no other way," she soliloquized, defending her actions.

She had been a wolf for too long to not know how they operate, the deer was used as a bait that would make the driver come down from the bus for them to attack before moving on to attacking the whole bus, killing everyone in it. While she felt bad for acting so heroic, hence making the presence of the only white wolf known, she knew it was for its protection.

"The white wolf must not die... no matter what." she reaffirmed to herself.

The three wolves were still lurking by the bush, but not as they were seen before. Like the white wolf, they had also transformed into their human forms. The wounded wolf now held on to a tree with his wounded hand to have a good view of the number plate of the bus.

"We've got ourselves company," he said in pain.

His voice sounded out of breath. If not for the fast healing ability of the wolves, he might have died of loss of blood. Two other figures, a young boy in his late teens and a much older woman in her early fifties, stood behind him waiting for the next line of action from him.

"Who was that little disrespectful white wolf?" the woman asked disgusted at the way the hunt went earlier.

"Whoever it was, it just cost us our breakfast," the man spoke in a more hoarse voice.

Nobody said a word after this as they were all still breathing heavily. After a few minutes of silence, the man spoke again.

"We need to know who our guest is," the man said, pausing to see the way the other duo would react. When none of them seemed to have an objection to this, he continued with what he had to say.

"Let's get to the bus depot to see if we can make out the wolf and greet him..." he stopped short as he looked at the woman among them.

"Or her to our town," he gave out a wicked grin.

"Shall we inform Manofield of the latest development?" the boy spoke for the first time.

The words were already out before he knew that it was the worst possible thing to come out of his mouth at that moment.

"And why would you do that?" the injured man who was in charge of the hunt asked as he moved towards the boy.

"He doesn't have to know anything," the boy corrected himself.

It was then, that the man stopped moving in his direction.

"If he finds out we were stopped by another wolf or that just a single wolf attacked and won against the three of us, he will be more than upset." He explained trying to let the young boy know why.

"And you don't want him to take his anger out on humans... or us, do you?" he asked.

The little boy shook his head. The man then looked up to the sky and was satisfied that the moon was still shining at its brightest. He transformed into a brown wolf with yellow and dark eyes and the boy and woman also did the same. He rushed towards the bus depot and he was followed closely by the other two wolves.

3
————

The depot was a large station where buses from many different locations dropped passengers going to Echo Cove. The light around it gave the feeling that the dawn had come quicker at the depot than anywhere else. Aside from the buses, expectant people were also hanging around. Some waiting to catch the first bus out of town. Some waiting for their loved ones. Then people carrying placards with names of people they were waiting for and finally those who seemed to be engaged with what she possibly did not have any idea of.

The bus arrived earlier than expected as the driver wanted nothing more than to get his job done and forget about the near-death experience he just had. Even though they were now at the depot where lots of people were, his face was still as cold and petrified like when he was face to face with the wolves.

When they all were out of the bus, Melody didn't look back to see other passengers. She could not stand seeing other people being reunited with their loved ones while she was without anyone and to make it worse she was not sure of where she was going.

She peaked at her white colored Samsung phone that had a wallpaper of her with the violin presented to her by the maestro when she graduated as a student. She swiped through the numerous applications on her phone but her mind was not on exactly what she was searching for, she let out a frustrating sound to get her mind back on track before she was able to get the GPS locator app on her phone.

She fiddled with it for a while to be sure of where exactly she should head to. As she didn't want to be looked at as a stranger with no knowledge of where she was going, and she knew attention was the last thing she needed to draw to herself so she took short steps in the direction she was facing.

She calmed herself to hear what all those around her were talking about but they seemed not to be saying anything of interest to her. She had grabbed her headset from the bag again to drown her raging mind in music as she prepared to follow wherever the GPS said when she heard something that made her stop short.

It first sounded like drunk people mumbling gibberish to each other but then, someone in the place mentioned an encounter with wolves and the people she had thought to be drunk started talking enthusiastically with the person.

"I think I found where to begin my search," she said to herself.

She began to follow the sound as she pressed the lock button on her phone to kill the light. She walked for about 10 minutes, passing shops whose owners were trying to get back to business for the day before she got to the place. It was a pub, with a blinking neon light that said "COMFORT,"

The door of the pub was made partially of glass that must have been broken in one of the fights as it paved the way for her to look through it. As she opened the door to enter, she felt warm air blow on her face. She moved in and kept looking straight ahead in order not to make eye contact with anyone. She was happy that the first place she looked turned out to be a perfect spot for her to sit as it was at the back corner very close to the window and it reminded her of her stay in the bus.

As she sat down her mind went back to the fight she picked earlier with the wolves and she knew the three wolves if not the whole pack just listed her as one of the most wanted because she broke the Wolf Code, but still, she prayed it would not be the case for her.

Judging from the things being spoken by the men in the pub, she realized that most of them were outdoorsmen. One of them was boasting about how many animals he had killed and that he was ready to kill as many animals as possible if allowed to. Another man in a bid to show off his profession also bragged about the number of trees he had chopped down and how he wouldn't stop till all the trees are no more in Echo Cove. As she heard this, she felt irritated and for some time, she felt like snapping their neck like a small twig with her super strength.

"I have a mission here, and it doesn't involve fighting or settling scores with anyone, not wolves, and definitely not humans," she mumbled to herself with her fist clenched tightly.

Unknown to her that a couple of people had noticed her entrance and one of them was standing in front of her, by the time she looked up with her frowned face, she felt disconcerted. She had not noticed the barkeeper approach her table.

"Are you okay?" the barkeeper asked her seeing the way she was looking.

The barkeep was a lanky man whose appearance depicted he had seen his share of violence as an unnatural scar was on his forehead.

"Yes I am," she answered him, comporting herself to look okay.

"What can I get you this lovely morning, ma'am?" the barkeep asked leaning to write down what Melody would say.

She thought for a while on what she would like to order, but eventually resolved to order any good thing that was advised by the barkeep that she had kept waiting for more than the normal time it took to take an order.

He disappeared to where he came from promising to blow her mind with the meal he would treat her to. But before he moved away, he turned around seeing something.

"You are new around here?" he asked her.

She looked up at him to see if anything was wrong but she could see the sincerity in his voice and his heart was beating normally.

"Is it that obvious?" she asked him, with a gentle smile barely showing her teeth.

"Hmm," the barkeep hummed for a while. "Of course. I am known not to forget beautiful faces and yours looks divinely carved." He flirted with her.

They both laughed at this obvious attempt at a pickup line and the barkeep thought he had made his score on her.

"You are a funny guy," she replied politely "But thanks anyway."

"Well, your backpack and map gave you up pretty easily," the barkeep later told her with a more serious tone.

"Oh!" she exclaimed as if she had totally forgotten about them. "I am actually a reporter from out of town, I am doing a story on a mysterious shaman known to be located in the woods around here," she explained to him giving him a broader smile to complete the spell.

The barkeep didn't say anything about this before he left to prepare the food. Growing up flirting was hard for her, mostly because she was a werewolf which was a major setback in dating humans, whom she had no attraction to whatsoever. She had to learn how to get them off her back while still being polite about it.

She had been asked out on dates countless times by random people and even her music companion but she had turned all of them down without giving them a genuine reason for it. Even Jason, who seemed like the closest human to her, knew he didn't stand a chance to win her heart. This was solitary lifestyle that was sometimes lonely for her but the wolf had always been there for her as a trusted friend and guardian. Thinking of the white wolf only brought her mind to the mission at hand for her.

In the midst of the noise inside the pub, she heard someone coming her way but she acted as if she was unaware of this. Then, the sound came closer to her. A man with a glass of wine banged it on the table she was in before taking a seat roughly. Even without her wolf trait, she could have perceived the horrible smell of alcohol oozing out of his body.

"I could not help but overhear you talking about that freak," he said stumbling at each word that came out of his mouth.

Melody knew better than to reply to him. She knew it would only be another long, unfruitful conversation that she could not afford to engage in so she shunned him, taking her gaze down towards her phone. Irritated by her action, the man stood up and dragged his chair near hers.

"Proving tough, huh?" he said with saliva coming out from all the corners of his mouth.

This time, Melody shook her head, hoping that would make him leave her in peace. The man smiled at himself before he leaned forward to her right ear.

"The freak is always sitting by the oak tree every night, creepy right?" he said. "So we are going to cut down that freakish looking tree. Call it a breakup," he spoke again now laughing hysterically.

The barkeep was in sight again but with a cup of coffee to keep her till the meal was ready. As he came in sight with Melody, she dragged her chair to the back to give her the chance to leave the drunken forester.

"I think I will be on my way now," she told the barkeep quickly.

Her heart was racing fast on hearing what the foresters had planned for Ishtar and majorly the oak tree - the one place that she had been visiting in her trance to visit the wolf for over fifteen years now. Surprisingly, before she could get out of the reach of the drunken man, he dragged her back but with swift reflexes and seemingly effortless movement, she turned the hand around as she spun giving her the chance to control his body through his hand. She would have broken his hands but that would have spoilt all that she had in the plan. So instead, she planted him back in the seat he stood from.

She didn't stop at this, she brought her eyes very close to the man's face and the man would have sworn that he saw her eyes changed. When she later released him, he didn't make a move to stand up again, all he could do was look at her as she walked away with her backpack.

Her breathing started slowing down when she got out in the fresh air, she walked down the street confidently as if she knew where she was going. She passed by a cop who was being radioed in the car.

"Be advised, three brown wolves were spotted near the depot," the female dispatcher on the other end of the radio said. "They are not in sight now but keep your eyes open," she said again.

She knew that it must have been the same wolves from the earlier fight, she looked around to see if she could see anything that could point her in the right direction as the map she had didn't contain the minor things that she might be in need of in this small town.

She started moving from one block to another knocking on anywhere that seemed like a hotel while she was able to speculate right on the motels, all of them were tightly booked for the day. Tired of how the search was going, she decided to go sit for a while at the local diner.

She was content seeing the diner was not as filled up as the pub and those there were all minding their own business. She took a seat at one of the booths. She felt lonely, disconnected and lost so she put her headset on so as to be able to discuss with her only real friend- the white majestic wolf.

Slowly, the world she was in began to fade away and in an instant, she was sitting with her back to the oak tree. The wolf aware of her presence walked slowly towards her. No matter the situation or the mood of the wolf, it carried itself in the most adorable way, its head was always held up high to make its yellow and red eyes more visible to see. It stopped, getting directly opposite her next to the tree.

"We are here," she said with a smile. "Where it all started. But what should I do?" she asked the wolf. "There are wolves on my trail... our trail just because we saved the driver and also everyone on the bus." She uttered again sounding confused and distressed.

The wolf didn't make any outward sign of panic about what she said, it moved closer to Melody as if to comfort her, it laid its head on her leg then a paw on her knee. And like she could read the wolf's mind, she heard the wolf talk.

"Take things one at a time. Wolves are always looking for a fight but you need to stay focus. The wolves will be dealt with in due time. I am here with you," the wolf said.

On getting what the wolf had to say, it rose up and gazed forward to another tree then back at her. Confused at its action, she also took her gaze in the direction that the wolf was looking before.

"Who's here?" she inquired with a very clear voice.

"That is Blaine," an unfamiliar voice said.

It sounded very thin but sonorous, even though it was low, it pierced Melody's mind stealing her concentration. As the world around her disappeared, it came back. She looked up lost to see a lady smiling at her.

"Pardon?" she said, trying to find a connection to what the waitress was saying.

She pointed towards a man that was at the door, not far from where she sat.

"He is the Forest Ranger of this part of town. And guess what?" she asked as she bent to face Melody. "He is the sweetest guy ever."

She gave a giggle as she took a seductive look at him. He turned towards them as if he knew they were talking about him and this made the waitress wave at him.

Truly, when he turned, Melody could see the reason that made the waitress have a crush on him. He was quite a handsome man, his broad shoulders were complimented with huge biceps. His dark and lustrous hair was combed to the back to rest on his shoulders. While his handsomeness was something that caught Melody off guard, his smile was the very thing that stole the breath out of her lungs.

Blaine on the other hand, as he was entering the diner was not looking at the lady that waved at him, it was the gorgeous lady sitting alone in the booth that caught his attention. He greeted and shook hands with anyone that was on the way without taking his gaze off Melody. Her beauty to him was flawless, even though her eyes showed stress and fatigue, her face was bright and her messy ponytail made her look like a coed a very attractive one at that.

He didn't want to judge the lady by her green tank top with a denim jacket on and distressed blue jeans but she looked like she was from the city and her whole composition depicted that she was lost and exhausted.

"Hello there princess," he greeted upon reaching her table, doffing his hat like a gentleman.

Melody, the woman who could shoot the advances of any man down at any point in time was completely dumbfounded when the handsome forest ranger got to her. All she could do was extend her hand slowly to him.

"My name is Blaine Chorus. I am the forest ranger in these parts," he introduced himself.

"I...I am Melody," she stuttered.

"It is an honor meeting you," he replied while he shook her hand.

He began asking if she was alright as she looked exhausted. Melody knew it was the time to drop her famous response that would leave the potential suitor speechless but what came out of her mouth was entirely different from what she thought of.

"I think you are right." she started talking. "I am here to study the illegal actions of the foresters, but it seemed the illegal activity here is not just cutting down trees." She said comfortably.

When asked what she meant, she narrated the ordeal she had with the drunk forester at the pub and how she had been unable to get a place to lodge. Blaine offered to help with lodging accommodations as his aunt had a room available in her house. Without a second thought, she agreed to stay there but Blaine excused himself to make a second confirmation.

He moved towards the door and gave Melody a comforting smile, as he held the phone close to his ears.

"Hi Aunt Marina," he greeted the person on the other line.

"What is it this time Blaine?" the woman's voice asked.

"I am really sorry about your tree, I will get justice for it." he first apologized.

"I have some good news for you." he started pausing to see what her response would be, but just as he thought it was cynical.

"I doubt that." she said emphatically.

"Well, I have got someone who wants to stay in your spare room.

A very sweet lady, she just got to town. And guess what?" he asked but didn't wait for her to reply.

"She loves nature as you do. She's here to put a stop to all of the illegal activities through her articles," he explained.

Upon hearing this, the woman's countenance changed entirely and she was more than happy to have her and also it will be another source of income for her as she lived alone with Blaine's little sister and cousin. They didn't talk much after this as he said his goodbyes before returning to Melody.

While he was making the call, he didn't know Melody could hear his side of the conversation. She felt the genuine kindness in his heart and this made her feel comfortable around him.

"The deal is sealed," he said on sitting down.

"All you have to do is wait here until I'm back from patrol and I'll drive you over... if that is okay with you?" he said while adding a packet of sugar to his coffee

Melody objected to this politely and offered to follow him instead so she would be able to learn the town and probably take a few pictures along the way. They ate the meal that had already been served while he was making a call before they headed out.

The sky was already coming to life as the sun was preparing to illuminate the horizon. An unexpected noise disturbed their conversation upon leaving the diner. A group of foresters were spotted bullying a young teenager who was protecting a woman from being leered at by them.

The group seemed familiar but she could not place where she had met them before until one of the foresters pushed the boy to the ground.

"You've just got a free ticket to Pain Park boy," he said.

The boy bounced up again which made the man shove him to the ground for the second time. Just as he stepped forward Blaine got hold of his hand and held on to it.

"Boys, we wouldn't wanna start our day like this, would we?" he asked them as he gently shoved him back against his group.

Melody could sense danger but didn't know where it was from, or if it was directed at Blaine or her. As she was trying to get a read on what the issue was, a very strong and calloused hand covered her mouth, the hand dragged her back to a secluded part of the street which was still dark from the shadows.

"You are one hard little wolf to track down in this two-bit town." He whispered in her ear.

He released her to see how she was going to react but Melody knew better. Picking another fight would not end well for either of them.

"Not so tough now, are you?" he quipped.

"Listen, I am sorry for what happened earlier," she first apologized to him. Then she noticed the wound on his face.

"And I am so sorry about your face. It will heal in no time," she said assuredly. "I just could not allow you to kill the driver or anyone else while I simply stood by and watched," she defended herself again.

"Oh!" the man said chuckling at her.

"The thing is... I don't like killing humans..." she was cut short by the man.

"Unless you have to right?" he asked her. He was sounding much calmer now.

She didn't answer the question. It was also the question she kept asking herself since she became a werewolf... whether she could or could not kill humans intentionally.

"Here it is, wolf," the man began talking again.

"No humans deserve to live, they are destroying our homes," he stated.

"That doesn't mean they deserve death," she fired back at him.

"I am here to warn you," the man spoke with a threatening deep voice as he moved closer to her. "Stay out of our way and tell your little human friend to stay clear of our business or else..." he also was interrupted by Melody before he could finish his statement.

"Or else what?" she flicked. "He becomes a collateral meal. Take this as a wolf courtesy." He said as he left her sight.

His words sent fear straight into her. She had just dragged Blaine into her mess unknowingly. The old man walked to where the boy was being bullied and challenged the drunk forester from earlier. But he declined to escalate the situation as he knew he was bound to lose.

It was then that Melody discovered his name as well as the other two who might have been the other wolves from the previous attack. Ryan was a strong man and was known to go to any length to protect his sidekicks... the boy's name was, Kris and the woman; Sage.

As the three of them moved away she could hear Sage asking if he had delivered the message and he replied affirmatively.

"Let's see what she will do now," he replied.

The fear was already leaving Melody as she crossed the road to catch up with Blaine. They entered the patrol car and sped off. Deep down, Melody hoped they got to the oak tree sooner rather than later.

4

Their journey to the forest was quick and they didn't say a word to each other until they got there. There was something about Blaine that Melody found very strange. In every human that she had ever seen, she could sense elements of evil in them but Blaine was different, it was as if he wasn't human. He was full of kindness and love. He parked the Range Rover patrol vehicle to the side of the road that looked like it had been frequented by cars.

"We are here," he commented before turning the key to kill the engine. "How about we split up, I will go inspect the forest while you look around to take pictures?" he offered. Melody looked at him and wondered if he was ever scared of the beasts that lived in the woods or if he even had any idea if there was anything like werewolves.

"Are you not scared of venturing into the forest alone?" she asked skeptically.

He chuckled before answering her.

"Of course not. There is nothing to worry about out there, the animals are innocent creatures they don't just attack and more so, it's daytime already so there's little to fear." he replied.

They both got out of the car and all Melody could think about was what Blaine said. The wild animals are innocent, just like the white wolf that was a part of her who was now faced with a life or death situation.

"I cannot kill an innocent animal," she thought to herself.

The sky was already bright enough for her to see around the forest, the sun rays were already touching the tall trees. She picked up her camera from her backpack before closing the door behind her. Blaine was no longer around as he had already ventured into the forest for inspection. The forest was cool that December morning, the falling leaves of different colors served as a plush carpet for the floor of the forest making it very beautiful. Also, the scanty leaves that remained on the tree had another level of beauty as the rays of light shone on them.

As she moved forward to take some pictures, she saw a very wide clearing, it was like being on a different planet where nature was not being destroyed. She could not tear her gaze away from the perfection that was spread out in front of her but a sound broke the charm cast by the clearing. She turned to see that Blaine was already back and was staring at her.

When he found out that she had caught him,, he felt embarrassed mostly for disrupting her moment appreciating all the beauty nature provided. He apologized immediately for this but Melody just smiled at him as she changed the topic.

"I once heard the foresters talk about an oak tree around here that was exceptional," she said.

"Oh, the famous oak tree. I can show it to you if you want." He told her.

She nodded in affirmation and in no time they were back inside the confines of the car again. He turned the car in the direction where the clearing was situated while he moved the car slowly past it through a narrow road. He stopped the car by this narrow pathway and pointed straight ahead.

"The oak tree you are looking for is over there." he said pointing to a well hidden path.

Melody got out of the car quickly and was almost running to get to the oak tree. When she got to the tree, she stood in awe and admiration. Although she had seen the oak tree in her many trances when speaking with the wolf and she knew the oak tree was a flawless creation to behold, what was in front of her was entirely different- it surpassed all that she could have possibly imagined.

The oak tree was very large, its bark was smooth without any bumps or imperfections, and none of its branches could be reached by mere hands as they were located up high. The height of the tree went up farther than the other trees around it and part of its root system could be seen around the forest and even past other trees. The mighty oak gave a sensation that they were standing at the core of the forest and looking at the mother of the trees of the forest. Blaine had also joined her where she was standing, he also took a moment to absorb what was in front of him before he spoke.

"I assume you know the myth that comes with this tree?" He spoke turning to see her response.

She shook her head as she has not heard of such. Blaine smiled at her before looking towards the tree again.

"My father told us the great legend that birthed the oak tree." He paused to allow Melody to take that in first.

"The tree was planted many centuries ago, long before my father or my father's father walked this earth as a symbol of peace and it was said that its guardian would guard the forest and everything in it," he told her.

She at first thought he was referring to the shaman as the guardian but she thought again that it could not possibly be him as the tree had been planted even before his existence. She decided to ask him.

"Who is the guardian?" she asked with a low voice.

"According to legend, it is said that the guardian is the majestic race of white wolves. But I don't think they exist anymore, we have not seen any of them around here in years." he said.

On hearing this, her heart sank. She had wanted to tell him that the white wolf still existed and the last of the legendary wolf tribe is at risk of dying but she couldn't. She also realized the reason she was always able to see the wolf at the oak tree, it was standing guard, fulfilling its duty not minding that it was the only one left. Her heart got more saddened at this.

"The foresters have no right to cut the tree down, it is a historical landmark for this town and..." he stopped on seeing the expression on Melody's face.

She was not just looking exhausted, she was looking pale.

"Are you sure you are alright?" he asked her.

She looked at him and shook her head.

"The room should be prepared by now, let's go," he announced, reaching over to take her camera bag from her shoulder. .

On getting inside the car, she thanked him for the help so far especially getting her a room to stay in. He smiled at her telling her he was happy to help. He drove out of the forest and went deep into Echo Cove.

THE HOUSE WAS LOCATED NOT TOO FAR FROM THE FOREST. IT WAS A very large bungalow built out of red bricks. The compound was filled with green grass that was kept low by regular mowing. As Blaine parked the car in front of the house an old woman rushed out. She met them just when their feet touched the ground, and gave Blaine a tight hug. Melody smiled at the love shown to him by his aunt when the aunt released him to do the same to her. Her chest lent warmth to Melody and she also returned the hug by holding on to her.

As if on cue, they broke apart and Aunt Marina's face was still beaming with a smile. His aunt was a woman who looked like she was in her late seventies with all her hair now white. Even with her age, her energy was like that of a young lady and the way she dressed was more evidence of her young heart. She had a pink flannel shirt and denim jeans on, which brought out her curvy hips.

"It is nice seeing you too," she said.

Aunt Marina walked her to the step leading to the door where they met Blaine waiting for them.

"Aunt Marina meet my friend Melody, the lady I spoke with about on the phone." He now turned to Melody, "Melody meet my aunt Marina." He introduced them to each other.

His aunt was more of a hugger as she hugged her again.

"Where are Sandy and Zane?" he asked his aunt as he held on the door for them to enter.

"Oh, they went to pick up something at the grocery store for me," she answered not saying precisely who went to do the shopping.

Upon entering the house, Melody looked around and she could see lots of pictures hung on the wall. Judging from the pictures, she knew that Blaine grew up with his aunt as the majority of the pictures were of him, two other kids and his aunt. Adjacent to the front door, the largest paintings were hung. It was a picture of a much larger family, while she did not know most of them, but she could point out Marina and a much younger Blaine.

Blaine sat on the fluffy brown couch near the fire as his aunt took Melody upstairs to where the room was. Judging from where they passed, the room looked more like a renovated attic but when they finally got inside, she didn't mind if it was once an attic.

It had been well arranged with the shelf and stood well-polished. The standing mirror was flanked by two tall shelves where she could put her bags and footwear. What made Melody happier than having the room to herself was that it had been painted green and she didn't care if it was already fading.

"I don't know your taste, but I hope you find this up to your standards," Marina said.

"I love it," Melody said with a calm voice.

They smiled at each other as she showed her where the bathroom was in case she wanted to freshen up. Marina then left her alone to do whatever she wanted to do and all Melody wanted was to sleep off the stress. When she was finally alone in her room, she looked around and pulled the curtain aside, before her was a large window that gave quite an entreating view of the forest. She smiled at the perfect location of her room and the color which made her feel as if she was living in a little cabin in the woods like the one she was laid inside years ago when she was only five.

She freshened up quick so as to take a nap but as she laid her head on the pillow, her mind went calm slowly like an ocean after a storm. For the first time in a long time, she didn't drift off to sleep with music although all she could remember of her last thought before drifting off was how to find Ishtar fast.

MELODY OPENED HER EYES SLOWLY, LOOKING AROUND HER, SHE FIRST felt strange but later her brain was fully functional to remind her that she was no longer in Uncle Donovan's place. This was her new home, with Aunt Marina and the others and she was in her own room in Echo Cove. She felt relieved and refreshed by her sleep. She didn't have any nightmares whatsoever about her parents and neither did any other actions that she had done in the past haunt her in her sleep.

She thought she had just slept for a few hours but when she looked through the large window in her room, she realized that she had slept from the morning until dinner time. She jumped off the bed and picked a sweater from her bag and changed into black leggings before going downstairs.

She heard sounds coming from the kitchen, she walked slowly to where the kitchen was and there, she saw Blaine's aunt moving about the kitchen trying to finish up the cooking in time and she was doing a dance to make the stress more fun. She had yet to notice her presence but she saw her when she took a spin. They giggled at each other. She waved at her to come into the kitchen.

"I wanna thank you for your hospitality so far. It really goes a long way," she spoke, as she did appreciate immensely.

"No problem dear," Marina told her.

Melody looked at the L-shaped counter that was in the kitchen. How Marina was able to keep it tidied up even while still cooking was a surprise to her.

"What can I do to help?" she inquired, willing to help the woman was a small way of returning the favor she had done for her.

Instead of saying something, Aunt Marina stood on a spot looking at her as if she had uttered something very terrible but it was not her fault. She had always been the one cooking without help although Blaine helped anytime he had any spare time but her niece, Sandy and even her son Zane, never made it their duty to help her out so she was very surprised at her offer to help.

She told her to go set the table for six people. Melody left the kitchen to prepare the plates and napkins on the table. While putting out the place settings, it made her feel as if she had a family of her own and just the thought made her very happy. She finished up with the task very quickly, just in time for Marina to finish up with the broiling of salmon and cooking the pasta. Marina finished cooking quicker with Melody's help and this gave them enough time for a little chit-chat.

Marina asked about her background and she relayed her story to her, but in order not to make her feel bad, she changed the topic.

"I couldn't help but notice that you are the only one I have seen since I got here," she pointed out what she had noticed.

"Oh, that is true... Zane is out with Blaine," she said. "You know boys, they are out playing football. And as for my dear niece, Sandy, she will be talking to one of her boyfriends on social media."

They were quiet for a while before Marina spoke again.

"To be young again, having fun just goofing around." now facing Melody, "Tell me, dear, do you have a boyfriend?" she asked her.

The question caught Melody off guard, as it had always been one of the questions that she dreaded answering for she knew answering negatively will make her second most dreaded question of why, surface.

"No, I haven't found the one that's right for me," she answered making sure her answer would answer her next possible question.

"Hmm," she sighed. "You sound like Blaine," she commented.

They moved on to the purpose of her coming to Echo Cove and she replied that she was doing a study on the illegal activities of the foresters and also to write a report on the legend of a shaman living in the woods." She said knowing that she might not be able to hide her purpose from the only family she seemed to have now.

"Ishtar," Marina spoke. "That is his real name, no one knows much about him but he will show up to help anyone in need and will just vanish into the thin air without a trace afterwards. I first thought he was a myth until Blaine said he had seen him before in the woods and I had also seen him vanish before my very eyes months ago." Marina told all that she knew about the shaman.

Melody wanted to say something but was interrupted by a voice.

"What a surprise," the voice said.

A young lady walked towards them as she greeted the two of them.

"It's not every day my brother brings home a girl," she spoke, looking over at Melody.

Marina saw how uncomfortable Melody was hearing this and she came to her rescue.

"Now, now Sandy, Melody is our guest." She "She is renting the room upstairs that is all,"

Sandy gave a disappointed look then leaned back in the chair she sat on.

"I wonder when this loser of a brother of mine will find someone good before he finally becomes a forest critter," she mumbled.

"Now, what was that?" Marina asked.

"Nothing," she replied sharply.

"What did I tell you about mumbling things when guests are around?" she asked her.

It was then that she apologized, but she was sure that what she said was heard by the two of them. She then looked at Melody again as if she recognized her from somewhere. But she didn't say anything as she could not pinpoint the precise place that she had seen her before.

The door flung open with force, Zane and Blaine came in with sweat all over their bodies and although Sandy and Marina might not be able to pick up on their smell from where they sat Melody could perceive the odor oozing out of their body.

"You two go get cleaned up for dinner right now," she yelled facing Zane in particular.

Zane rushed to his room to get himself cleaned after he gave a cheeky wink at Sandy on seeing Melody sitting there at the table, but Blaine on the other hand moved towards her. He became very coy with every step he took towards her, when he was close enough, all he could utter was a greeting and his face was facing downward while he greeted her. Sandy shuffled in irritation for the way her brother was acting like a dickhead. Melody was quite entertained with the way the family was acting and it made her realize what she had missed out on by not having a family.

In about ten minutes the two boys were back looking and smelling much cleaner and they all went to the dining table and sat down to eat. The dinner went quietly while they all had their fill. Melody thanked the whole house for their generosity before she told them she would like to go on a night walk to stretch her legs. All eyes turned to Blaine who was still battling with the bone in his hand. Annoyed by this, Zane kicked Blaine from under the table to spur him into action. The man couldn't take a hint if it came up and smacked him in the face. So sometimes Zane had to give a little nudge.

"W...would you mind me joining you? I need to digest all I have eaten." he offered sounding very nervous.

She nodded and they both left the house. Melody could sense that the whole house was looking at them as they moved away from the house.

"Yes, I am just gonna come out and say it, my brother is a fool," Sandy commented when they were out of sight but Melody could still hear her and this made her smile.

"What's up, you just smiled?" Blaine pointed out.

"Oh, just remembered something," she fibbed.

"What a lovely family you have," she commented. "I am usually the very shy type but I feel so comfortable speaking with your aunt. Your sister and cousin are very nice to me too."

Melody out of sheer curiosity asked about his parents and he gave the story of the tragedy that befell his family a long time ago. He told her that they died due to a fire set by some angry foresters who were sacked. His father was an environmentalist and his mother worked for an organization that helped with the relocation of endangered animals. And it was the reason he became a forest ranger

"They must have been good people. I am so sorry for your loss," Melody gave her condolences.

She also explained how her parents were taken from her when she was just five years old by a wild animal. Blaine stopped on hearing this and moved towards her. She looked pained and it was clearly because of what she just said, the pain was still haunting her.

"I am so sorry Melody. I could only imagine the pain you have gone through." He said with a gloomy voice.

Melody gave the look of pain again as she bent a little bit on the knee. Blaine took the moment, moved closer to her and placed his lips on hers. She also parted her lips just slightly. This went on for some time as she was lost in the kiss and to her, the world stood still.

Slowly, Blaine took his lips away as he apologized for being too forward but Melody told him it was fine. Melody still had the sorrowful look, but before he could ask what was really wrong, she asked if he could get the sweater she had dropped on the dining chair for her as she was freezing. He turned to go to the house immediately and she saw that he was no longer where she could see him. She let out her pain.

Truly, she was in pain but it was not because of what happened in the past but what was happening. She had felt pain in her right leg as if someone was trying to hit it with something sharp. She looked around to see if anyone was looking at her and when she was sure she was alone in the woods, she turned to a wolf. Without wasting the limited time that she had, the white wolf rushed to where the oak tree was located.

There, she found four foresters lying still very close to the oak tree with a chainsaw still running next to their eviscerated bodies. Their intestines were hanging out as if they had been pulled out inhumanely by wild beasts. She knew it was not just any wild beast but werewolves. She could smell their presence so she looked around with her wolf eyes. A few yards away, away from the sight of humans stood the three wolves she had seen earlier, Ryan, Kris and Sage and not only that, there was another wolf among them that she didn't know. She realized that they were from the same pack.

Not wanting trouble, she rushed back to where Blaine had left her shifting back to Melody before coming out of the bush. Blaine showed up minutes later with the sweater to see her leaning against a tree. He helped put the sweater on her and while at it he discovered a leaf tangled in her hair. He picked it out and showed it to her.

"Where did you get this?" he asked her looking quizzical.

"I don't know, maybe from the tree I leaned on or something," she replied sounding innocent.

"That can't be," Blaine gently objected to it. "This is a very rare leaf and it's not grown around here." He explained to her.

"Then it must be the wind," she spoke again.

"Hmm, that's far-fetched too. Only the oak trees have this type of leaf and its like four miles away," he looked more confused than before.

Melody not knowing what to say again gave a fake sneeze and Blaine suggested they go back home because of the cold. As they got closer to the house Blaine's mind keep trying to see the possibility of how she could possibly have the leaf in her hair.

"She couldn't have ran there, could she?" he asked himself knowing it was impossible.

Melody, on the other hand, was having mixed feelings, she was happy that the oak tree was saved and that it was the last day of the full moon but she hated the tactics employed by the brown wolves in protecting the oak tree. She didn't sit with the Blaine's family in the sitting room for long before she bade everyone a good night. As she went to bed she noticed that she had a cut on her lower ankle when she undressed. She treated it and while she knew the wound would be gone by in the morning, she added bandages to it to avoid staining her bed sheets.

She laid on the bed with just one thought.

"How is the white wolf connected to the tree?"

5
———————

It was the second weekend that Melody would be staying at Aunt Marina's place. She had been a sweet guest to them as she was quite helpful in the kitchen for Aunt Marina, a good influence on Sandy and a very huge crush for Blaine. Zane had been unable to fully accept her. All they have noticed was that she was jovial on matters that did not involve her past.

"What do you think of her?" Blaine asked his aunt one evening while he was alone with her.

"Who?' his aunt asked, acting ignorant of who he was referring to.

He looked at her in a funny but odd way then they both laughed for few minutes.

"I think she's a very good person," Marina answered him.

Even though she knew the meaning behind the question that he had asked, she wanted to make him work for the answers she knew he wanted from her.

"I know Aunt Marina," he replied as he was now sounding uneasy.

She smiled completely aware that she was already pushing him a bit. Blaine had always been a very shy person. Only his family had been given the chance to see the interesting parts of his personality.

He was usually at a loss for words when faced with someone he loved and this had affected his personal life quite dramatically.

"Have you asked Zane and your sister what they think of her?" Marina asked him.

He shook his head at this. He had seen her relate quite well with Sandy but he was not so sure of Zane. Aside from that, he could not judge on how they feel by how they related with her on the outside.

"Well, there is a silent tradition in our family," Aunt Marina started talking again. "Whenever we want to be sure of how the whole family might feel about someone, we will invite the person over to the lakeside," she stated.

She looked at Blaine to see his reaction. He had the look of disbelief in his eyes.

"That is just a suggestion though. It worked for me, and my siblings," she paused before she uttered her next words. "Even your father did this," she stated.

Blaine was quiet for a while about learning this fact, he was thinking of how that would make them bond. But having heard that his deceased father went through the same process, he readily agreed to it.

"But how are we going to invite her over?" Blaine asked with naivety clear in his tone.

"Oh poor child," his aunt teased him. "No matter how tall you've grown, you are still the same shy boy that fell from the tree years ago," she patted his hand in response

"You take your chance when it presents itself my dear. There is no us in this," she told him.

"How am I..." he uttered but the sound of the door opening made him stop to go check who it was.

His aunt followed suit too. Sandy and Melody entered the house laughing hysterically at something Blaine and Marina were completely oblivious of. They didn't say a word to them till they were done laughing.

"What could have caused you two to laugh that hard?" Marina asked quizzed.

"Oh!" Exclaimed Melody with her face still illuminated by her smile. "It was a..."

"It's just a little girl talk," Sandy cut in.

"That's good, I'm all ears." Marina answered.

She struck a pose with her hips swayed to one side like a model on a fashion magazine. This made the three of them laugh.

"What are you doing standing like that?" Sandy asked her brother who had spent his time standing there mute staring at Melody as she laughed. An inscrutable look on his face.

"Trying to capture the moment," he told her with a shy smile.

"Wait a moment, we will be going to the lakeside tomorrow," he declared facing Melody as he did.

You could hear a pin drop as everybody waited for what she would say.

"Oh, am I invited too?" she asked stuttering.

"Of course dear, you are family," Marina answered her.

"I'm in." she replied with joy.

She didn't wait for them to say anything else before she went up the stairs to her room, walking past Blaine with a smile on her face. He breathed deeply as she passed by him. Melody was wearing a perfume that smelled like apple pie. Blaine loved the smell on her. When she was no longer in sight Marina winked at him.

"Way to go dear, way to go." She said patting him on the shoulder as she left for her room too.

Sandy had already went back outside to talk to someone on the phone which was most likely a guy. Blaine was not alone in the sitting room for long before, Zane came in looking sweaty.

"Where are you coming from looking all sweaty," Blaine asked him.

"I was playing basketball with my friends," he replied.

"Who won?" Blaine asked him.

"Who do you think? I never lose," he boasted.

"Only to me," Blaine mumbled under his breath.

"What did you say?" Zane asked.

He didn't get an answer from him so he asked again, but instead of answering the question, Blaine said something entirely different.

"We will be going to the lakeside tomorrow," he informed him.

He stopped short to look at him in order to confirm if he was serious about it.

"With Melody?" he asked.

"Yes. Why?"

"I kinda like her." he answered him.

He ran to his room before his mother discovered that he was sweaty. Aunt Marina was partially mysophobic. Blaine smiled at himself for the reaction he got from Zane. He walked to his room too with the thought of what they would do to have fun by the lakeside aside from fishing.

Melody had been living a dream since she arrived at Marina's. She still had not wrapped her head around the fact that the family was caring and loving like she was one of their own. While her uncle Donovan was a very caring man before he passed away, he was unable to break through the walls of her heart like the Chorus family had. For the first time in her life, she was actually anticipating having fun with humans.

Melody smiled at the thought of her fishing and cracking all sorts of jokes with all of them. She was finally feeling happy for herself and the life she was living. But her joy was short-lived as a pang of pain from her side reminded her of what her reality was- she was dying. The sadness made her heart very heavy and she didn't know when tears began to form in her eyes. No matter the fun she was experiencing, it was just for a short period of time. Even her affection for Blaine could not stop her current pain of losing her only companion and then finally her life.

She tried hard not to make her sob be heard outside. The last thing she wanted was to drag the happy family into her predicament. Like she had always done during sad and lonely times, she reached for her earplugs to enhance her concentration to the astral journey to the oak tree. The Wolf was sitting at the opposite side of the tree without moving towards her but she felt peace and serenity staying there. In no time, she drifted off to sleep with the white wolf comforting her.

THE NIGHT WAS QUIET. IT MADE EVERY MEMBER OF THE HOUSE GET enough rest from the week's stress. It was the chirping of the birds and the sound of a chainsaw eating through trees that woke Melody up. On heading downstairs, she was surprised that she was the only one awake. She decided to get some things done before every other person would wake up, so she lit the electric kettle while she went about preparing breakfast for them.

The water hadn't begun boiling yet before she heard a footstep coming from behind. Before she could turn to see who it was, Zane spoke.

"I like you," he said to her.

A pinkish blush could be seen visibly on her cheeks and unintentionally she started stroking her hair to the back. She was quick to come back to her normal self.

"Good morning to you. I like you too Zane." she said.

It was the first time Zane would walk up to her to say anything. Most of the other times they had talked, it was either during a general conversation or when he didn't seem to have a choice.

"You wanna know why I really like you?" he went further.

"Hmm... I was about to ask." She said feeling good about Zane's little confession.

"Ask what?" Another voice joined their conversation.

Marina was surprised to see that she was not the first to wake up and also not the first person to visit the kitchen.

"I think my days of spending most of my time in the kitchen when I'm home are almost over," she commented moving out of the kitchen without turning.

She gave a wide smile and then winked at Melody before she disappeared.

"Your mom is quite funny," Melody commented.

"Most of the time," Zane added before chuckling wryly.

The whistling sound of the kettle brought Melody back to the reason she was in the kitchen that morning. Zane decided to stay back and help with the coffee while she attended to the breakfast she was preparing. He served everyone in the house a cup of coffee each. Sandy was the first to enter the kitchen with an empty cup. She was wearing a pair of over-sized trousers and a flowy blouse and her hair was left dangling. With just a glance at her, one would know that she had just rolled out of bed.

"How did you make this?" she asked holding up the cup. "I have never drank this kind of coffee in my entire life.

"I was about to say the same thing," Marina spoke as she too entered the kitchen. "But you beat me to it." now facing Melody.

"Melody dear, I am giving you all the coffee ingredients, please be my coffee maker. I would do anything to have a cup of that coffee before starting my day." Marina uttered jokingly clasping her hands together before her face.

"It's the least I can do," Melody replied.

The sweet coffee made that morning brought everyone back to life very fast. Sandy had poured the last of the coffee from the carafe while Melody had yet to finish hers. They were still all in the kitchen taking sips of coffee from their cups when Blaine entered the kitchen. He was dressed in a pair of brown shorts and a blue round neck shirt. He had leather sandals on with a bucket cap in one hand and an empty cup in another. He didn't expect to see everyone in the kitchen. Neither did he expect them to still be in their pajamas.

"Have we all forgotten what we planned today?" he teased looking at them one at a time. "And how did you make the coffee Aunt Marina?" he added.

They all replied like kids who got their birthday present earlier than the usual day. He was informed that it was made by Melody. On hearing this, his coyness set in, he moved closer to her at the other end of the kitchen. His eyes were fixed on her the entire time he crossed the kitchen.

"That was amazing," he complimented her on the breakfast.

She felt uncomfortable with his perusal. Her right hand partially covered her face while the left hand was on the kitchen table. It was Aunt Marina that saved them all. She reminded them of the lakeside hangout as she went off to get dressed and ready to leave. Melody also excused herself and she exited with Sandy.

"You know you are lucky, right?" Zane said

"I believe so," Blaine replied playfully. He caught a funny look from Zane. "Now, I know that look. Don't paint me as a larger than life person to her. Ladies always come around... they always do." he informed him.

Zane was already at the door before he finished his statement.

"Now you know a lot about ladies?" he jested, leaving him alone in the kitchen before he could utter another word.

Blaine looked around as he sighed. Then he left the kitchen too. Melody's mind was racing with joy and anxiety all at the same time. She had not felt him come close to her that much before. Truth be told she loved it, but it was not something she was used to- staying close with someone she loved so much. Upon reaching her room she began to scatter her wardrobe to get a suitable outfit to wear. She was still pondering on what to wear when Sandy barged inside. She had already changed to a plain white dress. She had in her hands other clothes she would want Melody to pick for her. She was surprised once she entered the room. It was the first time she would see her room so disorganized and also she had yet to get dressed.

"You aren't dressed yet?" she expressed her amazement.

Melody turned to her with a tired look.

"I am quite confused on what to wear," she told her.

Sandy moved closer to her. As she scanned the scattered clothes to see if her eyes would catch anything that she could wear at a glance. When she couldn't, she sat down beside her on the bed.

"I think we are exactly the same," Sandy uttered. "We always seem to be in a constant dilemma in picking the right outfit."

Melody looked at her surprised. She had always known Sandy to be the fashionista of the house and that was the last thing she expected to hear from her.

"Really?" Melody exclaimed to express her surprise. She leaned forward to see her face to confirm if she was joking. But her face was very straight.

"Of course, here are the shortlisted clothes," she announced. "I wanted you to pick for me, I didn't know you were also in the same boat as I was," she smiled at this.

They were silent for a while then Melody brought the idea of the two of them helping each other out with what to wear. This took about another twenty minutes but eventually they were all ready to go, Melody wore a fuchsia pink blouse to complement her chinos. Sandy also wore a similar outfit.

Zane, Marina and Blaine were already waiting for them to come downstairs. When they did, the two of them were looking like sisters. The compliment made the two of them comfortable in what they wore as they were still quite skeptical about it. They set out immediately and simply took their breakfast with them. Blaine and Zane had packed all the equipment they might need down at the lake, like fishing line and other things in the back of his car while all the food was packed inside the back of Marina's car.

The journey took about an hour. It was the place they always went to when they needed a break. But it was the first time Blaine would be there in quite some time. He didn't tell anyone of their true reason for them being there.

They were in luck as the place was not overly crowded. They took all that they would be needing out of the car while Blaine went to a shop at the lakeside to rent a boat. He was back with a key and they were ready to set off.

He helped with loading some of the things they planned on bringing and Melody did too. Blaine drove them to the far part of the lake. The houses around looked very tiny from where he stopped the boat. The sun was up but was not scorching. Marina took out some snacks that they all grazed on before they started hunting for fish. Melody didn't know how to go about this, but she was assisted by Zane with learning to bait her hook and how to cast her line out to prevent hitting the branches.

While he was busy teaching her, Marina called Blaine's attention to the pleasing way she was blending in and how the kids were happy with her.

"You know my boy is difficult to get to know, but I think he likes her," she told Blaine.

When she was done being tutored. They all gave her the chance to catch her first fish. She moved to the tip of the boat then flung the hook quite a distance in the lake. Nothing happened for quite some time, everything was calm. But as she turned to say something to Marina, the line shook once, then again. She had caught something. They all screamed in joy but she faced the lake reeling the line closer to her. The hook had caught a very big Salmon. Blaine helped sling the fish into the boat and they all applauded. Melody was overjoyed as she hugged them one at a time, even Blaine.

By evening, they had already caught about ten fish. The largest haul they had ever caught in a day. Although it was Melody's first time to go fishing, she got the hang of it faster than anyone had ever seen. When they were heading back to shore, Zane was watching the lake's movement and it caused dizziness to come upon him unexpectedly, he fell into the lake. They didn't catch what happened as fast as Blaine had moved, he made it a bit further before he turned. Before they got to him, Melody jumped into the river not minding what she was wearing. She picked him up with such agility, as they were hauled back into the boat by Blaine. They all laughed at this.

"What is a visit to the lake without partaking in some swimming?" Melody giggled.

They all laughed at the joke, even Zane who was out of breath, laughed at this. When they got home, they stayed outside to smoke the fish. Marina with Melody's help prepared Salmon sushi that evening. While they were cooking, Sandy was looking at her brother and how happy he was with the guest around. Since the tragedy of their family occurred, he seldom spent much time at home or even devoted much time to hangout with them.

6

It's been about 5 days since the lakeside experience. The dawn of every day brought along with it more attachment and fun with the family she was staying with. Everything seemed to be alright in her life. Most of the time, she would help Aunt Marina out with chores and when she was not doing that, she would be discussing girly stuff with Sandy. The conversation most of the time was about the town, the boys in it and then all the conversation somehow ended up with talking about Blaine.

As much as she had wanted to keep her affection for Blaine strictly to herself, their first kiss didn't help matters any, as she was always linking almost all their conversations back to Blaine. Sandy knew that she was fond of her brother too, so she kept painting him in a very good light, letting on of how terrified he used to be when speaking with ladies.

The time they spent at the lake, days ago, had also made the connection between her and Zane stronger. Even with him always going to town with Blaine or to hang out with friends, the little time they had together was always worthwhile. Bonding with him was not just the only thing now, it seemed them getting close had opened her to some things she didn't perceive at first. Since they had become proper friends, Melody always sensed danger anytime she was near him and her wolf sense had never lied or made mistakes, especially when it came to people that she cared about.

The sun was still up that day even though it was already getting later in the evening. It did not act as if it was tired of shining so bright. It had been a peaceful week for Melody as the Foresters had yet to be spotted in the nearby forest and the brown wolves seemed to have backed down, nothing brought calmness to her mind than these. Sandy and Melody were together at home, Zane was in town as usual and Blaine who typically used to be home by that hour was not. He was working late in town to supervise the preparation for the annual town dance.

While he was not mandated to be there, he had taken it upon himself to help out. It was the only place he could summon the courage and make plans on how he was going to ask Melody to accompany him to the dance. It was the first time he would be asking any lady out for the annual dance.

Having been stuck indoors for hours Melody was tired of being cooped up and she wanted so bad to see what the town looked like all decorated for the festivities, so she invited Sandy over to act like a wingman to keep the unwanted suitors at bay.

"Sandy," she called over to her. "Would you like to go shopping with me?" she asked making it sound like an offer more than a question.

"Are you kidding me?" Sandy leaped for joy. "Count me in and I know the best store in the whole town of Echo Cove that we can get all that you could ever want."

"Oh, so what is the store called?" Melody asked her knowing that the happiness shown by Sandy had more to it than excitement over a simple shopping expedition.

"Chic Chic," she replied.

Melody was quiet for a while to see if she had heard the name before.

"Is that the store where Chet works?" she asked hoping Sandy was going to reply in the negative.

Chet had been another topic they talked about almost every day. According to Sandy he was the most handsome guy in her age bracket and she seemed to be crushing on him hardcore and he was also having the same type of feelings for her.

Melody wore three-quarter leggings as well as a cozy shirt but when she got to the sitting room, she changed her mind to put on a sweater in case they ended up staying late in town. She also wore very comfy hiking boots and for the first time since she got to town, she allowed her hair to fall loose on her shoulders. Sandy wore a white crop top that had the picture of Barbie on it and a pair of high waisted black jeans.

"You look, classy girl," Melody commented as they headed out to the store.

The store was relatively small from the way that Sandy had always described it. She understood the reason for that assumption might be because she had yet to explore the outside world to see massive box stores like Wal-Mart. But aside from the size, the store was looking very modern. Outside the store was an electric horse that kids could ride on for just a coin and the huge front display window was well utilized as it was made to showcase the items that could be very useful for the upcoming dance.

On getting inside the store, Sandy hurriedly gave her the overview of the store, telling her where each of the departments were located. Without waiting to see if she had any questions, she rushed off to accomplish her main mission there- to see Chet; the checkout boy. After Melody had looked around to see where to get the things that she wanted, which were things that she didn't really need, she moved to the counter to check out the goods and also to see who the object of Sandy's affection was. The moment she laid her eyes on Chet, she was quite convinced that the term cute was accurate in describing him. His eyebrows were thick and his round eyes gave him a bunny kind of look-cute and cuddly.

She noticed that Chet was preoccupied with his discussion with Sandy so she just dropped the basket beside her to look at around other parts of the store to see if she could be tempted to purchase anything else. Her eyes caught something entirely different. She saw Zane walking around the store with some other guys who were looking rough and unkempt. She had wanted to ignore this as she knew a growing man could not be caged, but when she saw a familiar face among the boys her mind was instantly changed.

"I will be right back Sandy, I want to go say hello to Blaine," she said, knowing that she would not have heard her as she was totally preoccupied talking with Chet.

On stepping out into the cold atmosphere outside, she traveled the path that passed by the group of boys, but she kept at a distance where she would be unseen and yet she would be able to see all that was going on. The boys stopped at the corner of the store where there was a little reflection of light. The familiar boy among the boys was Kris, the little wolf who seemed stuck with Sage and Ryan. He lined up the boys in a single row as he stood in front of them.

He walked past them slowly like a general assessing the soldiers that he will take into battle. When he got to the front of the boys, he held his shoulders high. Melody not knowing what was about to happen moved closer using the darkness provided by the shadows as cover.

"Okay, which of you worthless souls want to become more than just a human sack of meat?" he asked pointing at the boys who were lined up in front of him.

None of the boys moved and he continued with his speech.

"One of you three will be given the honor to join an exclusive club where you will be treated as an equal. Where you will be more than human... you will become a God among men." He announced telling them of the accolades that awaited them if they joined up.

Melody could not believe her ears on hearing what he was saying. *"Is he trying to recruit new members to his pack?"* she asked herself.

She had not had the chance to see any other werewolves until she got to Echo Cove, but she knew quite well that this method of recruitment was the most awkward way of turning someone to a werewolf but whatever it was, she was not ready to lose Zane to the blood-thirsty werewolves of the town.

She looked around to see if she could see something that could be used as a tool for her to mess up their little meeting. No sooner had she gazed around that she saw a large rock, she smiled at it. She heaved the stone up and targeted Kris's side. She didn't want to hurt him but at the same time, she wanted to shake him up as well as the boys. The stone went up in the air, sensing the incoming weapon, Kris moved away and the stone hit the wall with an intense amount of force, crushing some bricks. Kris shivered in fear and when he looked around, he didn't see anyone. The other boys were more frightened at this sudden occurrence and they all started skittering away from the dimly lit corner before anything else could happen.

The stone crashing into the wall was what brought Zane back to his senses, he realized that the gang he was being invited to join might not be his thing and moreover, the stone might be a bad omen. He took a different direction from the other boys hoping that leaving alone would make him more inconspicuous to whoever might be watching. As he moved through the alleyway, a figure obstructed his movement. The man was quite tall, and he was wearing a black pinstripe suit and was also holding a cane whose head was made of a gold-plated wolf head. His hair was also dark curly and very long, almost at the same length as Melody's hair. His height was almost as tall as Blaine with his grey eyes staring down intently at the frightened Zane.

"Well, dear Zane, where are you going?" he asked with his deep voice echoing. This made him sound like the devil himself.

"I am heading back home. I am no longer interested in joining up." He said trying to shuffle around the man.

The man blocked his with his leg and gave him a wide wicked grin. He might have thought that would make him feel relaxed but it was achieving the opposite goal. It only served to set Zane more on edge.

Melody was watching the events unfold from afar trying to see how it would all play out as the man looked like the alpha of the pack that Kris belonged to. She thought of the best way to rescue Zane without vexing the Alpha when all of a sudden, she rushed over to where they were.

"There you are Zane," she shouted, moving towards him looking very happy and relieved to see him. "Where have you been, I have been looking all over for you," she added.

She walked nonchalantly past the Alpha and grabbed Zane's hand then turned him in the direction of the store.

"Go meet Sandy at the store she's expecting you," she told him, not giving him a chance to look back at the man.

Although she had been told numerous times that she was a bad liar, she hoped that the man wouldn't question what she just did and also that Sandy wouldn't show up outside the store laughing at a joke that was made by Chet. When Zane was safely away and out of earshot. She turned just in time to see that the man was now extremely close to her and his cold breath could be felt on her skin.

"I haven't had the chance to introduce myself." He said looking straight into her eyes. "I am Markus. Manofield Markus," he said.

He stretched his hand out to shake Melody's hand while his gaze was still locked on hers. Melody took his hand without breaking eye contact. This made them smile at each other but Markus didn't let go of her hand.

"What is a little wolf like you doing in my town? Where have you come from, little one?" he asked her with his eyebrow quirked in wonder.

Even though he was not happy seeing her after she had disrupted his conversation with Zane, he kept up the charade and Melody also was not interested in engaging in idle chit chat.

Melody looked ahead and was pleased to see Blaine heading their way.

"Don't worry," she said. "I am not staying here long. I am just here for a visit, that's all." She stated to him.

She pulled her hand gently away from him as she walked towards Blaine. Markus, on the other hand, turned to see her go and was full of questions, not for her but for his pack members.

"So a new wolf is in town, eh?" he muttered to himself as he palmed his cane.

"Funny no one remembered to tell me," he said grinding the words under his breath.

Blaine and Melody greeted each other with a hug, this was the first time they would hug since their first kiss out in the cold. They went to the Chic Chic store together and Zane was there sitting alone while Sandy was still wrapped up in flirting with Chet. Thankfully, she hadn't noticed a thing.

"Zane, I wanna show you something," Melody told Zane who followed her to a secluded aisle in the store.

"How about we forget about everything that happened tonight?" she asked him.

A spark of light showed in his eyes, he nodded once in affirmation and Melody continued her speech.

"But you will need to promise me that you will stop hanging out with any of those boys again. You are a sweet boy, don't trade that for anything," she said.

Zane agreed to the deal and hugged her for getting him out of a sticky situation. When they got back, Blaine had moved closer to Melody. And in a single breath, he rapidly asked the question that had been weighing on his heart for the past few days.

"Would you like to go to the dance with me?" he asked, trying not to make eye contact with her.

"It is a good way to know the town and it will...." he could feel his face growing warm as he continued to ramble on.

"...I would love to go to the dance with you." she cut in.

They both smiled at this before she rushed to where Sandy was, where she was laughing hysterically with Chet.

"Can I steal her for a moment?" she asked after clearing her throat to announce her presence.

"Of course," Chet stammered.

She pulled Sandy to the side to tell her that she was going to the dance with Blaine and Sandy gave a very broad smile at this. She knew her brother was already stepping up his game.

"I am going to need something to wear can you help me?" she later told Sandy letting her in on the main reason she was informing her.

"Oh. No problem with that." She said.

She hurried back to Chet and said her goodbyes, promising she would come by and see him soon. They all left the store and headed off in their separate ways. Zane joined Blaine in finishing up his work while the two ladies went to the boutique to find the appropriate dress for the dance.

Melody had thought that the store would have been the most impressive enterprise in the town for no reason at all but when they got to the boutique, her chest skipped a beat. It was quite large and made mostly of glass.

They started trying different clothes on but when they got serious about finding the right dress, Melody had to change into ten different outfits and five shoes before she was finally able to settle on a choice, a short black lace gown with a pair of flat shoes.

"How about this?" she asked Sandy as she got out of the changing room.

"This is perfect." Sandy complimented her "You don't really need me after all." She added with a grin.

"I am very happy to have you here, I needed a different opinion other than my own." Melody told her.

While she was changing into the different clothes, Sandy had called Marina to tell her the good news. Marina was overjoyed by this and had told her to take Melody to her favorite salon, promising that she would book them an appointment. They went to the Salon after the boutique and they were attended to by the best stylists there.

Although the dance was not till dusk, the town had already been painted red in preparation for it. Lanterns were hung at every corner of the streets and people were dressed in different attire and the music had already started. While the music was not the type she played as a career musician, she really loved it.

When evening came, Blaine had changed from his regular outfit of jeans and a casual shirt to a black suit that had once been worn by his father and it fit him perfectly. His hair was well styled too with gel making it sparkle. His heart literally stopped when he saw Melody all dressed up and the way her hair was coifed in loose curls. He had long doubted the power of the fairy godmother in Cinderella to make the heroine a perfect princess in such a short period of time but no more.

The dance went on until late in the night and they did their best to follow it through without taking a moment to rest. For once, she had forgotten how her life was going and in his arms, it was as if all her troubles had vanished. The hour was growing quite late when the dance finally ended, and she could see people heading off into the woods, not sure of what was happening, she inquired from Blaine. It was him that shed light on the tradition of the townspeople that they were going to the oak tree.

"After the dance, the oak tree is said to grant wishes of those who were of true heart," he said with a grin.

"I think we should go or what do you think?" he quickly suggested.

Melody nodded and they held each other's hand as they followed the numerous couples heading that way. When they got to the oak tree, people gathered around it with each one of them making their wish in silence.

Melody could sense the coyness in Blaine but yet was surprised that he held onto her hand all through the time he made his wish. When it was time for Melody to make a wish, she closed her eyes and placed her right hand over her heart.

"I wish to know where Ishtar is," she whispered her wishes so quietly under her breath,

The moment she completed her words, all the sound around her went away. She opened her eyes gently when she saw that the numerous lanterns that illuminated the forest before had been replaced by one light that was shining directly behind the oak tree. She opened her eyes wide and a man was standing in front of her.

He was wearing a funny looking cloak that partially resembled that of an Indian chief and it also looked like that of a Chinese sage.

A long beard had grown all over his face but his eyes had not changed a bit. In order not to make the wrong assumption, she moved closer to him.

"Are you Ishtar?" she asked him.

He nodded in affirmation of what she said, and then he looked beside her.

"I can see that you have taken really good care of her," he said nodding sagely.

Melody looked beside her to see whom his words were directed to and there the majestic white wolf was.

"What is it that you seek, my child?" he asked her, wanting to get straight to the task at hand.

She opened her mouth to explain her plight to him but as she tried to talk, she could only burst into tears. Ishtar looked at her surprised at what could be the cause of her tears.

"What troubles you my child?" he asked again.

"I am dying," she said still in tears. "I am dying day by day and I don't want the wolf to die with me," she told the shaman.

Ishtar felt sorry for the lady, he could feel her pain deep within his soul, as he had suffered much loss and rejection like her too. What struck his heart most was her selflessness and determination to protect the creature even if it would mean she would die. It was something she never believed to be humanly possible. He allowed her to shed a few more tears before speaking.

"There is a way," he said.

Abruptly, Melody stopped crying.

"If you want to set the wolf free, it is possible," he paused. "But you will need to bring the young man that obviously is in love with you and also has affection for animals to the temple of the elders at Coyote Rock 15 nights from now on the day of the red moon. It will be the day where the comet will fly over the earth and you must be there by the time the clock strikes midnight. It is the only way for the wolf to be separated from you and if this is not done then, the wolf will die with you," he finalized.

He looked at her to gauge her reaction, she seemed to be lost in her own thoughts. Her mind went to Blaine who in real life was beside her but completely oblivious to her discussion with the shaman. He loved her and she also loved him too and that was the first and perhaps only time she would ever witness love.

"Do you really want to do this?" Ishtar asked her.

She was silent for some time then looked at the wolf.

"I did not come here to find love or have a family. I came here to save the wolf and that is what I am going to do," she said with great conviction.

He gave her his blessing and then they spoke for a few minutes longer and he warned her of the Brown Billy Wolf Pack as they were brutal and ruthless in their dealings. But she informed him that her human form might be weak but her wolf part was still as strong as ever and if need be she would use force if dragged into their messy lives. They bid each other goodbye and Melody promised to see him again.

Blaine was not sure what was going on with Melody, she had been on her knees seemingly lost in thought for some time now so he touched her shoulder. She opened her eyes to the present world, her eyes still had tears shining in their depths and Blaine caught this.

"What is wrong?" he asked.

"I guess it is just the cold wind blowing into my eyes," Melody fibbed.

They moved on to the place where Blaine parked his car. When leaving, he looked back and winked at the oak tree, knowing no one saw him unbeknownst to him that Ishtar was watching them both intently.

"You are also of the pure heart. Your wish will come true. Time will tell, time will tell"

In a poof, he disappeared into the oak tree.

7

The day was bright as always, it was like Melody was on the different planet after the dance. It seemed the sun loved to shine its brightest onto the green grass and it made each blade practically sparkle to every eye that dared to gaze upon it. Having little civilization in a town had its own advantages too and Melody was enjoying the one she was having.

The house was dead quiet that afternoon, Blaine was off to work, Aunt Marina had gone out visiting a friend who stayed far away from town even her gist partner; Sandy had been busy with readings for the few tests that she would be having soon. Although she used to follow her to the library sometimes to do her own reading she decided not to follow her that day to give her a little breathing space.

As she walked around the house to see if she could find anything that would interest her, she found Zane sitting all by himself on the back deck and was looking lost and deep in thought. She stood there for a while hoping he would see her but when she realized that he was deeply lost in thought, she went back inside to make two cups of cocoa before coming back out and sitting by his side. He looked at her with gloomy eyes before turning his eyes away.

"Care for one?" she asked him raising one of the cocoa cups to him.

He looked at her then at the cup before taking it from her. Instead of saying his gratitude, he gave her a half smile. They sat for few minutes sipping from their cups in silence, when Melody thought it was right as she could sense that he was becoming more calm, she spoke.

"Why did you do it?" she asked him, making sure her voice showed emotion and was barely audible to anyone other than who it was meant for.

Zane didn't reply at first then he gave a loud sigh.

"I have always felt like an outsider in my family," he started speaking. "I have always been the weird one... Sandy is smart and she knows precisely what she wants out of life, Blaine is the town's golden boy and a great Forester and even my mother is happy in her own way but I..." He stopped for a while before moving on. "I am nothing. I do not have a place that I readily fit in to and I thought the offer from Kris would change everything, but I later found out that something was off that night."

He now faced Melody, "Thank you for helping me out of whatever that was the other day. I would have said that sooner but I felt kind of ashamed that you know," he said now smiling at her.

Melody, in turn, bumped her shoulder gently against his before ruffling his hair with her hands.

"What are friends for, right?" she asked as she took another sip from her mug of cocoa.

Then all was quiet again as silence descended on the deck. Since the day he set eyes on Melody he had fallen in love with her. She was beautiful and has a kind heart. Since he knew dating her was out of the question, he had wanted her for Blaine. They took the last sip from their cups at the same time and Zane offered to take the cups back inside and rinse them out.

Melody, who was now sitting alone, looked up and her mind went back to her experience at the oak tree. Then she decided to calm her mind by taking a walk. She informed Zane that she wanted to take a walk and she would be back very soon.

An hour after she had gone for the walk, she was yet to return. Even though Zane had told him the times she left the house, he kept looking up at her room. It was common for her to take a walk but staying out for over an hour alone was new to him.

"You are not her boyfriend," Blaine kept reminding himself.

His first thought was to head out to look for her, but he quickly talked himself out of it as he knew it would seem desperate and naïve to Melody and might even turn her off. So he decided to stay back but not long had he cleared his mind that his mind drifted back to her again.

"Could she have been disturbed by the foresters or even having fun with other guys?" he asked himself.

Since their kiss, he had been acting protective over her and he had never wanted to let her out of his sight. His heart was always racing when with her and no matter how often they saw each other, she always looked more angelic. He shook his head in embarrassment at the way he was acting, he thought about the time he didn't care about things like this and it was the ladies that would be worried and sick for attention.

"Guess its payback time for me," he thought to himself with a smirk.

He was still deep in thought when he caught a glimpse of Zane moping about. So he asked if he was interested in going fishing. Zane who was also tired of staying home quickly agreed.

Melody, on the other hand, had lost track of the time, she was enjoying the view and the alone time she was having. It gave her time to reflect and also think of her health, Blaine, and the wolf. Her first predicament was finding the shaman but now that she had found him, she was faced with another issue, of how she was going to bring Blaine to the Coyotes in just a few days.

As she walked by the bush to the direction of the oak tree, she saw a dark cave almost hidden from plain sight; she could sense the presence of something or someone watching her so she went to check it out. As she was unfamiliar with the cave, she used her wolf eyes to see through the darkness. It was not the first cave that she had seen since she got to Echo Cove but something about the cave drew her to it.

Not long after she started her walk into the cave that she started hearing the voice of a man, she was not sure before as it resembled the sound of falling rocks but as she moved closer, it was clear that it was a man yelling out loud.

The deeper she traveled into the cave, she felt the hair on the back of her neck tingle and it meant that the man and the people with him were not ordinary humans. She later got to where the man was and hid behind a rock so that she could see what was going on. She didn't find it hard to discover who the yelling man was. He was the one obstructing Zane the day of the dance, the alpha of the Brown Billy Pack. Melody quickly discovered what Manofield was mad about. He kept yelling at every werewolf his gaze fell on, rapidly questioning them on why he was not kept in the loop on the presence of a new wolf residing in pack lands.

"Who among you can tell me what type of wolf she is?" he yelled again and even the cave trembled in fear.

She also recognized three out of the pack, the same group of wolves she had encounters with since she got to town. They were not looking near as strong or confident as they looked the last time she saw them and they were awfully quiet. She knew that they knew all about her and her breed and she would no longer have the element of discreetness again.

"You," Manofield pointed at Ryan. "Tell me about the wolf. Now!"

Ryan narrated what happened that full moon to him, telling him that he was attacked without warning. Sage quickly defended herself and Kris by telling him that they were together so they didn't catch a good glimpse of the wolf. This confused Melody, as the three of them knew what she was. In her confusion, she had mistakenly made her presence felt as Manofield looked around to see if there was anybody in the cave that he did not know about. He stopped yelling as he spoke.

"Ryan, find out who the girl is and report directly to me as soon as possible." now facing Sage and Kris, "recruit more members to this pack will you?"

He gave them a stern warning that nobody should withhold any information from him ever again as it will only end in pain for any wolf that was caught. Melody seeing that Manofield had given the order to the wolves to search the cave took the path out of the cave and in no time was back on the main trail.

When she went into the cave, the road was empty but not anymore, a woman and a teenage boy were standing there looking at her.

"Sneaky rude wolf," Sage said to catch her attention. "Were you not told to mind your business in your pack?" she asked. "Oh! My bad." She said with a concerned but taunting tone. "You are the last of your kind," she added.

Kris all of a sudden grasped the joke and let out a loud peal of laughter.

"What is it you want from me?" she asked them crossing her arms across her chest not wanting to stay outside anymore.

"Manofield wants you to join our pack but I don't see that happening," she informed her in a very harsh and rude way. "Not that you are not wolf enough but one female wolf is all we need. We do not have any need for another woman in the group. No hard feelings," she told her giving her a wicked smile.

"None taken," Melody answered. "Listen, I do not want any trouble from you or anyone, I am not here to pick a fight or cause a mess. I came here for my own reasons," she calmly announced to them.

She tried to go on with her walk but was dragged back by Sage

"Where do you think you are going white wolf?" she asked.

"Oh! So you don't believe me?" Melody spoke now feeling quite frustrated with how the afternoon was going. "Here, take my hand, and tell me what you sense." She spoke loud and fast.

Reluctantly, she took her hand against her inclination. She didn't want to seem weak or scared of the white wolf especially not in front of Kris. As she grasped Melody's hand, everything was clear. She became very pale and cold. It was as if holding her hand was draining her life source and this made her let go of Melody's hand immediately. She stood and stared at her.

"This wolf is very sick. It's dying," she thought to herself.

"Are you sick?" she asked her with all the venom now gone out of her tone.

Melody looked away from her into another part of the bush as she answered her question indirectly.

"I came here to find Ishtar, to talk to him about what I am facing and if there is any way out of it without the wolf getting hurt." She explained before looking over at Kris then meeting her gaze again. "Now you see, until I can do the task I have at hand, I really do not want any trouble. I mean neither you nor your pack any harm."

Sage opened her mouth to talk but before she could spit out the words, Melody spoke again.

"Thanks for not telling him what breed of wolf I am," she expressed her gratitude. "But why didn't you tell?" she asked her.

Sage looked at her with a gentle eye then spoke very low.

"Leave, as quick as you can." she said softly under her breath.

"Leave? I don't..." Melody stopped talking to choose her words carefully.

"Manofield is a ruthless man and a violent wolf, whatever he sets his eyes and mind on, he will move heaven and the earth to get it, not caring about the collateral damage or who gets in his way." Sage pointed out to Melody.

"You have piqued his interest and now all he wants is you in our pack. So if you value your life and the lives of the humans around you... especially your boyfriend, you will leave town. It will take Manofield the work of a second to snap all their necks in just one hunt. That is why we didn't tell him what you really are. If he found out that you are the last majestic white wolf, you will have just increased the bounty on your head and increased the risk for your new found family." Sage gave a devilish smirk that scared Melody. But she regained her confidence in no time.

"See," she spoke slowly, her voice resonating with every syllable.

"You need to listen very carefully, I already told you I mean no harm to you but if anything happens to Blaine or his family, I will switch off my humanity and one at a time, I will take down all that you love and all that you have built, before I subject all of you to the most painful death you could ever think of," she threatened and her wolf eyes had replaced her black gentle eyes.

She tried to walk away again not long after relaying her parting words and this time she was not obstructed by Sage. She had made up her mind to go back home to see if everything was okay, as she knew the danger of threatening a werewolf. She had walked just a few steps away from them when she heard Kris finally speak up.

"She is right you know," he said in his tiny voice. "How come we did not tell Manofield what she really is?" he asked innocently.

Sage turned to him with a smiling face which made Kris unsure of why she was smiling.

"We didn't say anything my young apprentice, because we will deliver her to Manofield ourselves and we will be recognized and given a commendation for this," she said.

"It is a full moon tonight," Kris told her.

"Then tonight, we have a wolf to kidnap," she said grinning wickedly.

8

———————

Melody's fast walk had quickly morphed into a run in an instant. She knew werewolves by nature, were not time wasters, if they wanted to do things, they quickly acted upon it. The time that she was not around to protect her family could expose them to a much greater risk of becoming victims of a brutal attack and to make matters worse, it was a full moon tonight. She would have wanted to shift into a wolf so as to tap into the great speed fully, but she could not risk having her identity more exposed than it had already been with the Brown Billy Pack. Her heart was racing faster by the time the house was in sight, but another fear crept in as she approached the house – she could neither hear any sound coming from the house nor perceive any signs of life inside.

Once inside, she checked every room but it only confirmed her initial deduction.

"What could be wrong? Where could they all be?" she asked herself.

She raced to where the home phone was and beside it was Blaine's cell number written boldly on a book. She typed the number in quickly and held her breath waiting for the call to connect. Nothing came out of the phone at first and this was already frustrating her. Then the sound came.

"Hi there," Blaine said in a bright voice but as she went to answer him, Blaine's voice spoke again.

"I am not here right now so leave a message but if it's urgent..." his voice cut out for a while before restarting "...still leave a message. Have a good one!" he said with his voice full of life.

Melody dropped the phone angrily on the table.

"Stupid voicemail," she murmured.

Not knowing the next thing to do, she stroked her hair to the back as she turned towards the window. She had wanted to move towards it when the phone rang, her heart jumped as she picked the call quickly.

"Hello!" she said almost in tears.

"Hey, it's Sandy. Are you alright?" she asked concerned with the way Melody answered the phone.

Instead of answering her question, she threw the same question back at her. Sandy answered affirmative to this and she explained to her that she would be staying over at a friend's house to do more studying and answer group discussion questions.

Melody didn't care what her reason for staying over was, she was happy to know that she was safe. It was also an advantage to her as she didn't know what evil lurked around the family and in case the wolves decided they wanted to attack they would not know her location.

"Will you let my brother know when he makes it back?" Sandy asked her, knowing that she was not attentive to her.

"Ooff... Of course, I will tell him when I see him," she replied stammering.

Sandy was about to say something about a guy that she met that day when Melody caught the scent of someone lurking around. She quickly cut Sandy off as she said her *adios* and dropped the call without waiting for her reply.

Although she was sure of the person whose scent she caught, but she stood still for a while to see if her nose or ears could pick up on something more. The last thing she wanted was to walk into a trap but when she could not hear or smell anything more, she trailed the scent gently and discreetly. The scent led her to the driveway and it stopped. She looked on the ground and she saw tire tracks that would have been made not long ago. She knew only one person could be reckless to leave such a mark- Blaine. She deduced that Blaine must have been home earlier than usual today and maybe took Zane out as he was the only one at home and she could smell Blaine too in the garage however faint the smell was.

With no one but her home, the house stood still and quiet and the only sound she could hear was due to her enhanced hearing and it was coming from the bees who were trying to suck the nectar of some flowers outside. She dreaded the silence, as she knew it would be worse if the wolves got to her new family before she could help them. Her eyes started welling up with tears with the series of bad thoughts, then she remembered that regardless of what happened, she would not be alive long enough to witness it.

She caught the scent of Blaine again and she followed her nose to where it was leading her. She was pleased that no one was around to see her sniff out the scent, as she knew that she would only be suspected of being a weirdo and not a supernatural creature.

The scent took her into the woods then a clear path till she reached a place that used to be the stream but the December weather had frozen it into a solid sheet of ice. From afar she saw Zane and Blaine fishing. They had already caught two medium-sized fishes. It was a great haul for them, as the fishes that would normally be in the stream would have swum deeper into the river to avoid the icy part.

Blaine knowing the unstable nature of the ice river had persuaded his cousin that they should stay on the dock to catch whatever came their way.

"Hey Blaine," Zane called out to Blaine breaking the long silence between them.

Blaine was not much of a talker and he was like the oddball in the family full of Chatty Cathy's, and if there was one thing that Zane could not stand; it was staying somewhere without moving his mouth. Blaine looked at him as he made a sound without opening his mouth.

"Do you think Melody is going to stay around?" he asked him.

Blaine could only look at him, as he had yet to give the right reply for his question. It was a question he had also been contemplating for a very long time since he discovered his affection to Melody.

"Wait! Why are you asking me?" he asked skeptically but all Zane did was give him a very quizzical face with his right eyebrow raised higher than the left. Blaine got the message that he wasn't fooling anyone, least of all Zane.

"Is it really that obvious how I feel about her?" he asked and Zane nodded to confirm that.

"How obvious?" he asked again.

"Like the sun shining high in the sky," he answered him.

Blaine heard a sound coming from behind them and this made him stand up quickly and he ordered Zane to do the same. They looked around but didn't see anything.

"Maybe you are just imagining things because we were talking about your girlfriend," Zane teased.

When he looked at Blaine's face, he knew he was not joking as his face was as serious as ever. The growling sound came again and it was audible to Zane this time. He had never had the chance to see a wild animal not protected by iron bars before and this made him remember all the bad things he had seen in movies on how wild animals will attack humans in cold blood with little provocation and tear them apart. Under the evening sky in the bush very close to the ice covered river, two pairs of yellow eyes burned furiously. The bright yellow eyes also gave light to the grey part of it which made the sight of looking at it more chilling than whatever they wanted to do.

The two wolves jumped out of the cover of the bushes and began to move towards the two men. Blaine knew what they were driving at so he turned to Zane.

"Zane, I need you to be a very brave and strong man right now. I am going to distract them and while I do this I want you to head straight to my SUV, open the driver's door and at the corner, you will see my rifle. Get it and bring it here quickly." He ordered him.

As the wolves advanced towards them, they also took few steps to the back. On getting to the edge of the dock, Blaine guided Zane down onto the river as he also went on the ice using his foot to detect the weak spot so as not to fall into it.

Zane made a break for the SUV at the same time that the wolves reached the dock. As he ran past them, they just increased their growl and did not follow him. It was this that made it clear that they were there for Blaine and him alone.

Surprised at this, Zane looked back to see what the beasts were about to do to Blaine but as he turned, he lost balance and slipped on the ice making him tumble down the hill before his head slammed hard on a rock that was covered with snow. His eyes first went bright but as fast as the light came, he blacked out.

Melody was watching from where she stood on the path so when she saw Zane passed out and his blood staining the white snow, she felt nauseated but with all her might she subdued it. She could smell the blood from where she was spurred on by the fear that something terrible might have happened to Zane she rushed to where he laid motionless, she slapped his cheek to see if he would regain consciousness but, as he didn't. She calmed her mind enough to smell her environment and she could perceive humans close by. She turned to a wolf immediately to make a very loud howl to the moon. She did it again to be sure that the humans nearby heard it. When she heard their footsteps coming that way, she hid in the woods to see them take care of him before running to the dock to check on Blaine.

The wolves were still taunting Blaine but they had not caused him any harm. They kept stalking him as they eagerly awaited their prize. They were already in the middle of the lake circling round Blaine, their large teeth were out and growling low in their throats to add a more threatening sound to their growl.

On seeing the state that Blaine was in and knowing without a doubt that the two wolves were Sage and Kris, she decided to return the favor they gave her that evening. She stood away from them to give a loud growl as a warning but her growl meant nothing to them as they continued to stalk him.

"Have it your way then," Melody thought as she dashed fearlessly onto the ice. Although she was running with great speed, she was being very careful not to step on the weak spots of the ice. When the two brown wolves saw this, they prepared themselves for her arrival but Kris not wanting to lose the fight again for the pack broke rank and charged towards Blaine instead, she pushed him to the ground, making him land on his side.

Melody was furious at this and her speed doubled, and Kris charged toward her with super agility but when he got to Melody, he found out that his strength was nothing compared to hers. It was as if she had unlimited strength and nothing could beat her. She used her front paws to scratch his face before pushing him hard backwards.

Sage seeing this moved fast to attack the majestic wolf as well, she opened her mouth in preparation for biting a portion of Melody's body but as she got near, Melody weaved to the right, dodging Sage's teeth. Before Sage could recover from the lost attack, Melody had grabbed her by the neck when she let out a distress call to the rest of the pack. Annoyed with the cowardice showed by Sage in calling for help having outnumbered her, she, with great force picked Sage up with her teeth and flung her away. She landed a few feet away from Blaine crashing head first on the ice. She looked around for Blaine but didn't see him. She bent to catch his scent and she could feel him close by but his scent was muted.

She forgot the fight in an instant as she looked through the ice to see if she could locate him. The next image she saw sent fear straight to her heart. Blaine had fallen under the ice and had no way to get out as the ice had closed up again. She started jumping on the ice hoping it would break but it didn't.

A look at Blaine showed that he had just a few minutes left before he would die either of hypothermia or suffocation as his eyes were already heavy and were drifting closed gradually. The distress call made by Sage got Manofield and Ryan rushing to the scene and they saw the fatal blow that had been dealt to Sage.

She didn't care who else had joined them on the ice as she continued jumping on the ice. She looked around to see if she could see anything that could be of help when her eyes caught a tree at the riverbank that was already crooked. She made a quick run towards the tree and slammed her body against it to see where its weak point was. Upon figuring out where she needed to strike the tree she ran back to the ice and charged the tree again. She did this three more times till the tree gave way and fell on the ice.

Immediately, the ice broke apart and Blaine was able to raise his head up to breathe but he couldn't stay above water long as he was completely exhausted. Melody knew that there was little the wolf could do for him now so she transformed back to herself quickly as she jumped into the cold water to haul him out. Since she learned how to swim against her wish while with her uncle, it wasn't until that day that she actually got to appreciate it.

The surface was quiet for some time before part of the ice river broke again with two figures coming out of it. Manofield was watching all this and was very surprised that the lady who saved Zane the other day was the majestic white wolf. As she was struggling to save her love, a sudden thought occurred to him.

I want her in my pack, I will make the majestic white wolf as my bride, he thought to himself before he gave a wicked smile at his thought.

The tree that shattered the ice had already made all the ice weak so the Brown Billy Wolves barely made it out of there with their life. In her human form, she dragged Blaine off of the lake but still out of breath, she discovered the mistake she had unwittingly made.

While struggling to get Blaine out of the lake, she had unknowingly brought him to the other side of the lake. On figuring this out, she laid her head on the ground exhausted from what had already happened. She turned back to the majestic wolf and ran around the bank that they were on to see if there was a way for them to get to the other side where the Jeep was parked but it was all blocked by debris and snow and ice. She returned to where Blaine was dejected, as she could not risk taking them both over the ice again. To make the situation worse, snow had started falling and this alongside the near-drowning that Blaine just had made him barely conscious and he was at risk for hypothermia if she couldn't raise his body temperature quickly. She knew that she had to get him to safety if she didn't want to lose him. She moved his body farther away from the bank and turned him to his side. She bent her neck and wiggled under his body then with force, she heaved him on her back.

The majestic wolf was moving slowly with the added weight on her back looking for a safe place they could rest till the snow stopped and for him to get warm. Fate smiled on them as she found a cave not far from where they came ashore. She increased her pace in order for them to reach the place faster as she was also getting tired.

Upon reaching the cave she dropped Blaine against the entrance of the cave before going around the cave to search if there was any other creatures in there with them. She could not smell any presence and from the looks of the cave, she deduced that the cave had not been used for a very long time. The numerous sandbags and tarps that had been covered with dust gave the impression that it was once a mine.

Once she was sure that only the two of them were in the cave, she turned back to Melody as she began to carry sandbags, placing them on top of one another as she placed the tarp in the middle then the ground to form a fort around her and Blaine. She put what she had learned as a member of the Girls' Guild into practice as she struck two stones together to create a spark to start a fire on some tarps she had placed on the ground.

When the fire was burning strongly, she began to undress Blaine, taking off his shirt first then his black drenched undershirt. She pondered if there was a way to get him warmed up without removing his pants so she could maintain his modesty. But she quickly came to the conclusion that it was impossible to achieve that if the cold cloth was not removed, so she unhooked his belt before she removed his long brown pants. When she had finally accomplished stripping him naked and covering him up, she was breathing heavily, she didn't know that stripping off wet clothing would be harder than it looked.

She placed him beside the fire to get warm while she undressed too. She felt uncomfortable doing this in front of Blaine even though he was not really conscious. She pulled off her clothes and placed them on one of the sandbags. She turned slowly towards Blaine and remembered that it was her first time to be completely naked in front of any man not to talk about the love of her life.

She walked closer to Blaine lay on top of him before she put some tarps on top of her to cover the two of them. She had read it somewhere that the body heat from humans can help warm another in the case of cold when out for a hiking or a forest camp. She stayed on top of him for about ten minutes but saw no improvement in his temperature and instead, his breathing kept decreasing and his face kept turning pale and lifeless.

"I don't think I have enough heat to sustain the two of us," she thought to herself.

She knew that it was time to bring another entity to help them out. She closed her eyes and gently brought out the majestic wolf but instead of turning into a wolf, she remained herself but with all the wolf's abilities at the forefront.

The first time she had done this was when Ricky, a bully in college tried to have his way with her. The wolf wanted to intercede by coming out to defend her but as she was just about to morph, she stopped it. So instead of her being the not so strong Melody, she brought out the powers of the wolf while she maintained her physical appearance.

She felt the heat coursing through her body increase so she laid on him again and the heat started having an effect on him. Melody's thinking had been blocked by her thought to save Blaine at all costs that she forgot the nature of the wolf- whenever she was in the wolf form, all she felt would be heightened, and a simple moment of anger as a human could become uncontrollable rage when she turned to a wolf. So when she brought out the powers and ability of the wolf, her affection and love for Blaine was increased.

She took a look at Blaine's still body and her emotions went off the charts quickly. She looked at his lips down to his well-formed body and he was no doubt a man that any sane lady would desire. She remembered the first time they kissed and how fulfilled and happy that made her feel.

"What in the world are you doing?" she thought to herself.

But it was just a thought. She started crying however knowing that she was bound to lose Blaine either way. If the cold of the raging storm didn't kill them, the cancer that she was battling would.

As she wept, Melody's eyes coincidentally turned from the normal color that Blaine knew to yellow then as quickly as it changed it went back to being her normal eye color.

She realized that Blaine was partially conscious so she closed her eyes, absorbing the moment as she let out her emotions in tears. But as soon as the wave of sadness reseeded, she felt so good being wrapped around Blaine with his heartbeat sending a reassuring message to her. Melody would do anything to stay like that for all eternity with him but then she remembered the doctor's words.

"You have only a few months to live, considering the level of your cancer," the doctor had said.

It was as if the doctor was there with them, she closed her eyes tightly, and a single teardrop found its way out of her eyes again.

"If only love could solve anything. If it could only be strong enough to cure my cancer," she thought to herself.

Gradually her thoughts drifted to her mission at Echo Cove, that she was there to free the wolf and not to allow her selfish desires to disrupt it.

"I guess getting the fairy tale happy ending is not meant for everybody," she thought again as she drifted off to sleep in Blaine's arms.

9

______

The once beautiful view of Echo Cove was totally covered with white, the snow kept falling and didn't look as if it was going to end anytime soon. With the storm raging on outside and its freezing breeze, no ordinary human dared to go outdoors.

Zane was very lucky to have been found by some kindhearted foresters who made their way to the hospital just moments before the storm blanketed the town in a carpet of white fluffy snow. Since it was a small town and because of the critical condition that he was in, he was granted admission to the hospital before things got out of hand.

All the bumpy movement and noise just to revive him first proved futile until he started regaining his breathing slowly. This happened after he had been subjected to series of electrical shocks to attempt to get his heart restarted. The doctor gave a sigh of relief on seeing him respond and even though the ward was cold, the doctor could be seen breaking a sweat, as it was his first time to ever attend to critical emergency since he graduated from medical school.

During this period, his head wound had been treated and bandages were being wrapped around his skull. When he fell, the force had also fractured his left ankle but it was straightened and placed in a cast while he was unconscious. As the doctor looked over his handiwork, a nurse broke his moment of silent happiness to alert him to another trauma that was incoming.

At the opposite end of town, in a cave that was lit with a mildly burning fire which was trying to stay alive with the cold air that was finding its way into the cave.

Blaine broke into a smile as he opened his eyes. When he looked at himself, he was no longer wearing what he had on before. He was wearing a white suit that had a yellow flower attached to it, a flower that was commonly seen around the oak tree.

He was not sure of what was happening to him, as he could not remember how he got to where he was. When he thought of this, he looked at himself.

"Where am I?" he soliloquized, then he turned to see if he could decipher where he was.

He was quite familiar with where he was it was; his room. He decided to go out of the room with his nice suit that was complemented with a brown Italian brogue. His hand was about to touch the knob, when the door suddenly opened up.

"What have you been doing inside since morning?" Zane shouted at him.

Like him, his dark hair was styled and it looked as if it had just been cut by the barber. He had a black suit on with a white flower. He was looking very happy but a little tense at the same time. When he realized that Blaine was still looking as if he was lost, he gave him a weird look with one of his eyeballs bigger than the other.

"Why are you looking at me that way?" he asked quizzically at the way he was acting. "You look like you just seen a ghost." he started laughing hysterically at the way he was looking.

"I have always known you to freak out, you even dread people talking about this day to you but this was more than I expected." he teased again, now punching his tummy softly.

Blaine, being a forester whose parents had died when he was young had only a few things that he feared and fewer things that he dreaded people discussing, his brain began to conjure a list of things that Zane could be talking about but he just couldn't come up with a plausible explanation.

"What is going on?" he asked Zane looking completely lost.

"I am so going to tell everybody about this," Zane spoke again and all of the sounds around Blaine went eerily quiet.

"Wait!" Blaine's mind screamed out loud.

"Suit, neat and well-polished shoes, a flower on my chest."

He looked over to Zane who was still saying something that he couldn't hear, since his own thoughts were louder than any sound outside it. He spoke out loud in the realization of what was going on.

"It's... it's my wedding?" He spoke slowly as realization began to dawn on him.

"Of course it is. You did it bro and I am so happy for you." Zane said now helping with his suit to make it hang right off of his shoulders and handed him a pocket square.

Blaine wanted to say something to Zane but as he opened his mouth, another person walked in. the person was wearing a dark blue suit, he had a mustache whose end looked funny as it curled right back to his nostrils.

In a glance, one would see the collar around his neck and the large bible in his hands.

"Blaine, meet Bishop Simon," Zane introduced the two men. "He will be the one to tie you guys together." He said.

Blaine looked at him then moved towards him slowly shaking his hand.

"Hi, Bishop, thank you so much for coming." he greeted.

"No Thanks necessary my child," the Bishop said even though it seemed more like they were around the same age.

"The archbishop sends his congratulatory message and also his apologies for not making it down here as he had promised," The Bishop said when he noticed that Blaine had not let go of his hands and was not saying anything, so he spoke again.

"The Lord's work can be unpredictable, as I'm sure you understand." he uttered.

"Yes, indeed," Blaine managed to say.

"Good, people are arriving outside so let's go and get you married," the Bishop said with a loud joyful burst of laughter.

The both of them walked out of the room together to the large lawn in front of their house. Blaine was not sure of what to think or what to even say. When they got outside, he could see that a very wide part of it had been decorated with different colors of clothes, flowers, and a variety of balloons were also attached to the tents. As he walked down to the front with the Bishop leading and Zane following along behind him, people kept waving at him and shouting a congratulatory message to him.

When he looked to his right, he saw Wendy, the woman who broke his heart years ago saying he was good for nothing and would not ever get anyone to put up with him. She was waving at him and he would have sworn he saw her wink at him.

Although he didn't know what was going on or how he got there, seeing that Wendy was at his wedding and even acting in a regretful way made him love what was going on. He smiled to himself and he also waved at Linda, the lady that worked at the diner.

When he got to the front of everyone, he turned to the crowd who were seated in the chairs in front of him and their gazes were all on him. All of a sudden he was not feeling too good about what was going on, his gaze traveled over the crowd assembled until he saw his aunt as well as Sandy who stood up as he turned fully.

They were wearing a very long gown that had a silver bead attached to its end, the look of his aunt in high heels and makeup shaved what appeared to be twenty years off her age. They were smiling at him and Sandy gave him a thumbs up. He smiled at this.

"What a crazy family I have," he thought to himself, then his mind turned to something it had omitted before, someone who was in their family but he had not seen yet.

"It is a great day today," the Bishop spoke dragging him back to the present.

Then all of the people seated rose up on their feet as they turned to the opposite side of the tent, the place they passed when they were coming. Then the bride was heading his way, his heart began to beat very fast. His aunt was already beside him by that time and as if she knew what was going on with him, she held on to his hand, this seemed to calm him down but one question struck his heart.

Who is the bride?

He squinted his eyes to see if he would be able to see through the white veil that covered her face but he could not. He also noticed that no one was following her but when he tried to guess her identity once again, he saw something that was disturbing.

A white wolf was walking serenely beside the bride and he was the only one that looked confused and a bit scared by this.

"Are they not seeing this?" he thought to himself.

When the bride got to the front, the wolf had already disappeared so he thought it was his mind that was simply playing tricks on him. The Bishop started giving the normal sermon for the service but all he could think about is who could possibly be behind the veil. He was tapped by the Bishop to say his vows, and when it was the Bride's turn, the voice gave him all the answers he wanted.

"You may kiss the bride," the Bishop said.

He smiled to himself, as he now knew without a doubt who the bride was. As he moved to lift her veil, a noise distracted him. The noise was coming from a place very close to where his aunt was sitting. Then, the sound of breaking tables was heard on another side. People were running away and taking any possible way out of the tent. After looking perplexed for some time, he saw the reason for their noise.

Four brown wolves were scaring people away showing their large teeth and clashing them together to show that they could easily eviscerate any of the wedding guests if they stepped out of line.

"Kiss me," Melody said from the veil. "Kiss me now Blaine," she said again this time her tone was bordering on authoritative.

Blaine looked at her confused, then he looked towards where the wolves were again, they were not moving very fast in their direction. They might be able to escape the chaos in the tent.

"We need to run," Blaine said gently when he discovered that nobody was still in the tent, not his aunt or his sister but as he tried to go run with his bride, he saw that the white wedding gown was lying on the floor and the white wolf he saw earlier was growling behind him. Melody was nowhere in sight.

In fear, he rushed out of the tent, but instead of seeing the house, he fell and by the time he opened his eyes, he realized he was lying naked by a fire inside a cave waiting for the storm to die down. He had an excruciating pain in his head and he laid back on the tarp-covered ground thinking back over his dream.

In the midst of the storm the white wolf could be seen scavenging for food, Melody knew Blaine just had a little time left to live if she didn't take any action. Even with all the power she had as a wolf, the white wolf was still struggling with survival out in the wilderness. But she was determined to do whatever it takes to make Blaine survive the whole mess with the least trauma possible.

"I won't lose him," she growled to herself as she ran against the storm.

It was as if nature was against her that day as it seemed the snowstorm was getting much worse with every step she took away from the cave.

A few miles opposite where she was trying to get to town, the cave where the Brown Billy Pack used to have their meeting was well lit with fires burning at every corner of the cave. All of the wolf pack was there, moving up and down in silence as they awaited what the alpha wolf would say.

He had been unusually quiet that night and none of them could speculate on what could have caused him to just sit with his back towards everybody with an indifferent look and thoughtful attitude.

Sage was scared especially since Melody literally tore her throat out in their last encounter, luckily it was not serious and her throat healed itself. His silence was justified out of the fact that she talked Kris into attacking the wolf that later kicked their asses or he was just mad at himself for not killing the wolf that night instead. She knew Manofield was so many things and one thing he wasn't was forgiving. He had managed to chase all other species of werewolves away from the town and killed those that refused to leave. The truth was that

Manofield had power issues and could do anything to prove himself to be superior and she loved that about him- he was a ruthless leader.

As she was still thinking of what could possibly be wrong with Manofield, he stood up and looked around him. He could see the anxiety in the way they all looked at him. They stood still without any expression on their face in order to make anything out from what he had to say. They could not afford to make the mistake of looking happy or too angry that day as he could snap their neck in anger.

As he looked at them, then he did something that was least expected of him, he gave a very mild smile. Kris looked at Ryan and Ryan, in turn, looked at Sage. They all had a confused look as to what Manofield could have thought of to have elicited that smile. But they all knew that the smile could only mean one thing; he had devised a more diabolical idea to kill the white wolf.

"I warned her," Sage thought to herself before Manofield started to talk.

"The white wolf has deprived us of our meal tonight," he started talking, allowing time for himself to swallow a lot of saliva that one could hear him gulp down.

"And it was for the second time if I am correct," he continued his impassioned speech. "But I have devised a way to solve our problem permanently." He smiled again.

"We all know that the majestic white wolf is known for its vast power, endurance, and speed. We all know the destruction the black wolf did to reduce their number to one and it cost them all their life. We won't do that. I am smarter than our brethren." He said.

"Instead of fighting the white wolf and losing our lives in the bloody fight, I will take her as my own and her power will be passed round to all of you, my pack." He laid out his plan.

His pack members looked at him as if he had just said something that was not only least expected but something that was completely ridiculous in every sense.

"What do you mean, take her as your own?" Sage asked not wanting to believe her ears.

Manofield looked at her then spoke with a straight face.

"I mean take her as my own in every way possible. I will take her as my mate," he said. "It will set us above all other packs and then we can branch out all over the town and country." He stated simply.

Sage kept quiet and even though she might not mean it, her face showed disappointment for the alpha who was legendary for his brutality and ability to strike fear into the heart of their enemies. But as it was with what she just heard Manofield say, she knew he was no longer himself. He had grown soft but she was not sure if it was Melody's beauty and innocence that he found attractive that made marrying her look like it was for the greater cause or because he feared being beaten by the white wolf. But regardless of what the reason might be Sage knew he was no longer the leader she signed up with.

"It is time for us to be the pack of packs. We... the Brown Billy wolf are destined for this. It is our rightful destiny." Manofield declared raising his voice to make his words hit hard with his audience. Kris moved backward from where he stood with a smile, but Sage stood her ground.

All Ryan did was look at him and how he was laying down his plans, he knew what it meant to him. Although all he was saying was technically for the good of the pack he also knew it meant more than that. If not for that night that he went to inform Manofield in his house on their raid years ago he wouldn't have known the main reason behind his craving to possess the white wolf.

His mind went back to that summer when he went to Manofield's house to give him the report. He found the house in perfect silence as he didn't hear or smell any creature of interest around. When he knocked, the door went ajar by itself so he decided to snoop around the house since Manofield hated seeing people in his house and was secretive about where his family was.

He went to what looked like his bedroom and on the bedside table, he saw a picture frame of his younger self with his parents and other kids that were mostly his siblings. He looked at it for a while and wondered what could have happened to the little kid smiling with so much energy in the picture. As he turned to leave, his eyes caught on a shelf where he thought would only contain clothes. When he opened it, he didn't see any clothes as the compartment of the shelf was made like a bookshelf. He saw lots of books with no titles written on them so he removed a volume from the shelf and began to flip through it and it was within the pages that he read all the deepest thoughts of Manofield since he was a kid.

He was born to an always-angry father who complained about all the actions that he took. He was always comparing him with the kids of the neighbors and even when he was very convinced that he could excel in any sport, his father's words always served to bring him down.

His father was just half the problem, he also was constantly bullied in school by seniors and classmates alike. His mother should have been the one to help him out during times like these, but she was also silent every time issues came up, and the only advice she would give was for him to stop being a loser and be better.

All of his childhood was spent alone trying to prove himself to no avail and this had made him an angry person with not just his family or schoolmates but with humans in general. His greatest gift was being a wolf when he got to college and at first, he was still seen as a loser. The Willow Wolf-- which was an organization in college secretly meant wolves hated him and the fact that he was turned by mistake by a reckless nomad wolf made them seek out to end his life.

The many incidents had left him with lots of wounds and he had to come home to treat himself. Instead of being received with love and care from his family, he was nagged and spoken to in all manner of disrespectful ways. A night of the full moon passed when he was in the hospital and it only served to heighten his emotions and he broke out through the window and in rage, killed his parents leaving his little sister to run away.

While their death gave him peace from their nagging, it didn't prove that he was not a loser. And since then, he had been trying to be the most legendary wolf ever known on earth, this was the reason why he could not allow the existence of other wolves in the town.

The reason why he needed to win Melody over, so as to make their bloodlines stronger.

He was feeling very hyper on telling them the plan as if he had a secret he was not telling them and this made Ryan ask him

"Do you have a plan to accomplish that?" he asked the Alpha.

"Winning a woman over is easier than fighting a white wolf," he told him still in a very jovial mood.

"I don't think we need her to be strong," Sage finally spoke her mind. "She might be strong but we can take her as a team, as the powerful pack that we are." She uttered.

"Of course we can take her head on, even though the chances are slim and aside from that it would cost us more than we bargained for. So why waste innocent lives when we can be stronger and better without suffering from anything?" He argued subtly.

He stopped to look at Sage before talking again.

"Oh! Is that jealousy I smell off you? Desperation does not suit you in the slightest" he asked rhetorically before laughing hysterically.

"Don't worry about that. You are still mine too," he spoke in a deepened voice that matched the storm outside the cave.

10

The night was longer than it was envisaged. The myriad of wolf tracks all over the town had been covered with loads of snowflakes and one could barely move around the white dome that had covered Echo Cove. The weather had been working in favor of Sandy and her friend Samantha as they were enjoying the heater and warmth provided by the big blanket they had.

Their enjoyment had been obliterating by a single phone call however. It was a call from an unknown person, although she later found out it was from the hospital.

"Hello there, I'm trying to reach the family of Zane?" a female voice said from the other side of the call with her tone depicting worry.

"Hi, who is this?" Sandy had asked not sure who the person was.

"I am Amanda, I am calling from the hospital." She introduced herself.

As Sandy heard this, her heart began racing very fast and all she could think of was her family. She knew by that time, everybody would be home aside from her aunt who was not in town. She didn't allow the caller to utter another statement before she rained down a series of questions. The caller allowed her to say all that she had to ask before giving her a single answer that would clear the air.

"It's about, Zane," she declared in a clear voice, as she didn't want to repeat such sad news. "He had been badly injured and was rushed here by some foresters." She said again.

Even though the woman was still speaking, it all turned gibberish in Sandy's ears as she was trying to connect the dots. She knew Zane would either be home or with Blaine, so hearing that he was hurt and brought in by some unknown foresters made her wonder where her brother or Melody was. So, once again, she decided to ask for the whereabouts of her brother but just as she went to ask, the line went dead.

As she dropped the call, Samantha knew that something was wrong, as her friend's once smiling face and bright blue eyes had been replaced with a horrible frown that displayed all the frown lines on her forehead and her eyes had also turned red with unshed tears. In all, she looked like someone who had never tasted happiness before and it scared her deeply.

"What's wrong? Who was that on the phone?" she asked her friend even though she could detect from the conversation that the person calling was from the hospital.

"Zane, he's...hurt..." she spoke gently, moving closer to her with her phone still held tightly to her chest in shock. "An accident occurred and..." she couldn't finish her words before she broke into tears.

Her friend moved closer to her to comfort her, after a while Sandy composed herself, and she told Samantha she needed to go to the hospital.

"The storm is still crazy outside, how am I going to get a cab in this weather?" she asked herself loudly.

"That, I can help with," her friend said with a smile.

She exited her room to go ask her parents for help in getting Sandy to the hospital. She explained all that had happened and with them being considerate, her father resolved to take them in his car. She rushed back to her room to see that her friend was dressed and prepared to leave. She had let herself into her wardrobe to get a black cardigan and parka.

"You are prepared," she said with a smile trying to lighten the mood.

"I cannot afford to lose any more time," Sandy replied with a weak smile.

In no time, they had got into Samantha's dad's car, a black Toyota Camry that bore the name of the company he worked for. He was a swift driver, as he knew how to navigate the snowy road without being blocked by it. They could barely see outside but they were lucky that he knew how to use the fog lights very well.

The drive took about thirty minutes, as they had to go in a very slow manner in order not to cause an accident. He had barely parked the car when Sandy rushed out of the vehicle not minding if she would get wet. It was the security guard at the door of the hospital that blocked her entry to the hospital.

"Is everything okay ma'am?" he asked politely.

"Let her enter," a familiar voice told him and he stepped aside to allow her entry.

She whispered her appreciation to no one in particular.

"You must be Sandy," the woman said with a smile. "Zane was right about how you were going to react," she smiled.

Sandy on hearing this knew the woman was the same person she spoke with on the phone. She began to direct her to where Zane was resting.

She entered the ward he was admitted to slowly and tears began to fill her eyes, Samantha, and her dad were already following along behind her at the time. He was gently squeezing her shoulder to give her courage.

"He is getting better now," the nurse said. "But we shouldn't disturb his rest. Shall we?" she said turning back the way that they came from.

Quietly, they all went to the waiting room. Sandy didn't know precisely what to think about it as she had yet to hear anything from her aunt, brother, or even Melody and she didn't have an idea what they might be going through or if they even knew what was going on with Zane.

"Where was Blaine when this happened to Zane?" she asked herself as she sat on the hard chair in the waiting room facing another agitated face who clearly had a loved one in the emergency room.

THE MEETING HAD JUST ENDED WITH MANOFIELD, HE WAS TOO JOYOUS that night but clearly he wanted this plan to be carried out the moment he had spoken.

"Ryan," he had shouted. "I am giving you the chance to do what you know how to do best," he said moving closer to him to speak quietly to only his ears.

"Wreak havoc. Do whatever you have to do to bring the white wolf and the filthy human she was protecting to me," he ordered as he moved back laughing like he had officially lost it.

Ryan who would have loved the idea on a normal day was caught off guard when Manofield added that he wanted to start the search immediately.

"But... the storm," Ryan spoke, subtly, protesting

"Which do you fear most, the storm... Or me?" He asked and all of a sudden, his face changed from the happy madman to a grumpy old granddad.

"I will start the search right away," Ryan declarad as he went to start the search.

He shifted to a brown wolf immediately, he growled then howled before running out of the cave. Even after he had gone, his howls were still reverberating across the wall of the cave.

The storm had increased in intensity from the last time he saw it, and it made him wonder if Manofield would not have given him that kind of order if he knew the current state of the storm.

"He wouldn't care," he thought to himself as he moved slowly into the storm with no clue to follow as the heavy snow had covered all the tracks, he could not even see his paw prints within minutes of leaving a place. He occasionally would hide behind a tree for him to see the closest to him.

Even his nose was useless in the storm, the only smell he could perceive was that of himself and the decaying leaves and trees which had all been subdued thanks to the impact of the snow.

"It is going to be a crazy night," he thought to himself.

Sage and Kris who stayed in the cave with Manofield had shared the same emotion with Ryan and they were doubting their leader. They had decided to stay in a secluded part of the cave away from Manofield as they do not know what his next order might be.

"We caused all this," Kris lamented.

"What do you mean?" Sage asked him even though she knew what he meant by that.

"We decided to attack that man so we could get the white wolf but she overpowered us," he stated.

Sage looked at him, disgusted that he tried to rub her face in their failure without even a care in the world.

"Have you heard of the rhetorical question before?" she asked, trying not to flare up.

"If we had defeated her, we would be worshipped and adored by everybody." She told him.

"But now, Manofield wants to marry her," he added.

Sage was quiet about this as she also never saw that particular development coming, her mind went back to when they were fighting in order for her to forget what was wrong and it was as if Kris was doing the same thing as he began to talk about it.

"How come she is so strong?" she asked. "I bet if Manofield took her head on, he would be defeated. "It was as if she was three wolves combined in one." He continued to chatter incessantly.

"And she's sick," Sage spoke quietly.

"That is not even what surprises me. I found out about her power the day I saw her charge Ryan in front of the bus. I have never seen anyone make Ryan surrender in combat." Sage paused to gulp before she went on with what she had to say.

"What surprises me the most is the wolf and that man. Their bond is not one I have seen before. She was ready to go to any length to save him. I have never seen a wolf act so unbeastly. I think she had mastered something we have never." She pondered the relationship those two shared.

"What is that?" Kris asked confused at what she said.

"She had learned to control her wolf side. She has learned how to allow her beastly side to be in harmony with her human side." She explained to him. "And that ability gave her even more power over us," she accepted.

She looked towards Kris then suddenly broke into tears.

"I almost lost you today." She broke down, holding him very tight to her chest.

He also let out his emotions but was still acting discreetly as they didn't want to draw the attention of Manofield. They sobbed for some time before they broke apart.

"The human is a strange person as well," Kris uttered as he wiped the tears from his face.

"Yes, you are right," Sage agreed with him.

They began to speak of how he had shown a greater love by helping Kris up, not minding in the slightest that he was once attacked by him. They spoke of how Melody and Blaine were like peas from the same pod and it made Sage wonder if Manofield would have shown the same compassion they saw for his pack members, especially her.

Although Sage and Manofield had been involved before, they both with silent agreement did not speak of it and it made Sage burn from within and wonder if he still had the same kind of affection for her or if he was actually done with her. But regardless, she was not ready to lose him to anybody, not even the majestic white wolf.

They all waited for the storm to die down and Melody luckily had found an abandoned cottage. She was sure that the owners must have evacuated from the storm that night abandoning the cottage, as she could see that the food she found was still fresh and the wood from the fireplace looked freshly burnt.

She took all the food she could carry inside a large blanket, putting it on her back then she changed back to a wolf and ran back to the cave. Getting back to the cave was easier as she was not running against the storm this time. She was relieved to hear Blaine's heartbeat from the mouth of the cave. He looked like he was resting more comfortably and she was also happy that he would not be able to see her in her wolf form.

She took a glance at him as the majestic wolf before she started turning bigger till she was fully back to being Melody. She prepared a bowl of soup for herself and Blaine and when she waited for him to wake to no avail, she began to get worried and decided to feed him even in his sleep.

He took the meal from her spoon by spoon in his half-conscious state without having an idea of who might be feeding him or where he was.

11

───────────

It was now the middle of the night. The sky was still heavy with snow clouds and it seemed like there was no end in sight for the wintery precipitation. Manofield, tired of hearing what Sage and Kris were discussing, stood at the mouth of the cave to see the current state of the storm.

When he realized that the storm had subsided to a gentle snowfall, he shifted to a giant wolf and gave a very loud howl. The sound got to Sage and Kris and they also transformed to their wolf forms as they rushed towards where their leader was but once they got there, they found out that he had run into the woods and they could barely catch a glimpse of him before the fog deterred them further. Kris wanted to run after him but was obstructed by Sage.

"If we are needed, we will be called," Sage said gradually changing her form back to human.

Manofield was running very fast without showing any sign of weakness caused by the harsh weather. His breath echoed heavily as he raced through the trees not paying attention to any smell that his nose might have caught. When he saw a wide field up ahead, he gave a growl of relief and he decelerated at the same time. He started walking slowly towards the popular oak tree whose leaves were very few.

Since he was very young, he had been told the stories of the oak tree and the Great Spirit that lived inside it. Even though it sounded more like a bedtime story, he as well as some people in the town had seen proof of the existence of Ishtar- a shaman who lived in the tree and was bestowed by the gods to know everything. He had thought of who could help in his quest and in answering some questions he had sparked a memory of when he first met the shaman. He had decided to try his luck with the shaman.

By the time he got closer to the tree, he moved around it for no reason, he also waited a while to listen to the sounds of the woods all around him. He could neither smell nor hear anything out of the ordinary, he bent a bit lower to the ground and gradually, he began to rise again until the shape reached the full height of Manofield. He looked pale from the cold that raced through to reach the tree.

Not so far from the oak tree, on the same path that was taken by Manofield stood Ryan, who was becoming dejected and tired of the search he had embarked on hours ago. He would have loved to go back and stay in the comfort of the cave or his house but he had never failed in his search before and he was not planning to start now. Especially when Manofield had tied the fate of all the pack members to it.

The only improvement that had happened was that the storm had weakened, paving the way for him to scent trails and it was the only thing that he could bank on for the search. When he walked down the path, scratching and sniffing the ground for clues, he saw a print on the snow, it was almost fading, but he could have never misread the mark. It was a paw print of a wolf.

"A wolf passed here not long ago," he told himself, feeling new energy fill his body in preparation for hunting the wolf who owned the paw prints.

He began to trail the print quickly in order not to lose the clue. He thought of who the print might be for and knowing that he left all his pack members in the cave, he could only come to one conclusion- it must belong to the majestic white wolf.

Ryan tracked the paw print to an open field, upon a glance, he knew exactly where he was. It was the location of the famed oak tree and he was quite sure that the wolf would be there. He moved slowly towards the exact place that the oak tree was located, but as he saw it from afar, he saw a figure in front of the tree.

At first, the thought it was Melody but after a second look, he noticed that the figure was stocky and huge, so it could not possibly be for a female shifter. Another thing that caught his eyes was the clothing that the person wore, he looked very close to see who it was and then he connected the dots.

"What the hell is he doing here?" he asked himself.

He flanked right into the bush not minding the snowflakes that drifted down onto his body, he moved towards him so he could hear what he was saying and at the same time see exactly what he was doing out in the cold alone when he clearly did not express any mission he planned on undertaking before he left him in the cave.

"What could he possibly be doing here?" he asked himself again.

Like Manofield, he had also heard the stories of the spirit man called Ishtar who lived in the oak tree, he was known as the protector of the forest and had found a harmony between himself and the animal of the woods who had all come to know him as a friend. Few people had only seen him and most times when people wanted to see him out of sheer curiosity, he would refuse to show himself.

Not much time had passed before Manofield began to shout at the oak tree.

"Come out Ishtar," he screamed, "Show yourself, I know you are in there," he continued.

He waited for a while and then he shouted again and this time his voice was more thunderous than before and it was a bit similar to the wolf's howl. Instead of anybody replying, it was the bird of the sky that trembled in fear of what the human beast would do to them if he decided to vent his anger on them.

After shouting for some time, a dark shadow was seen behind the oak tree and this made Manofield move backward. Then, slowly the shadow moved further out of the tree to its front and there Ishtar was. A man who had been given the power to know everything, do everything but would not act against the normal order of nature. Seeing the old and ragged Ishtar, Manofield remembered the tales he once heard about him he had also been given the gift of immortality.

Ishtar stood straight to see who had come to disturb his peace and the peace of the whole woods. When their eyes met, Ishtar recognized him immediately and knew the reason why he was there to see him.

Manofield's heart skipped a beat as his eyes met with those of the great shaman, it was not like any other eyes that he had gazed into before. It was not just looking into his eyeballs but was as if it was searching his soul.

The shaman approached him and sniffed all around before moving back, as if he was taking his measure.

"Why do you disturb our peace?" Ishtar asked him with a voice that neither expressed being pleased to see him nor anger.

"Do you know who I am?" he asked Ishtar.

"Yes. You are Manofield, the alpha wolf of the Brown Billy wolves. Destroyer of the furless wolves," the shaman spoke without any inflection given to his words.

Manofield smiled as Ishtar spoke these words not taking heed to the contempt with which he was saying it.

"Why are you here Manofield? What is it you need?" the shaman asked him not wanting to stay long with the wolf than was absolutely necessary.

While he got out of the tree, he had first thought that Manofield was the only one there but the moment he stepped out of the shadows he felt the presence of another but had decided not to utter a word about it. Manofield looked at him for a while and wondered if all the stories he had heard about him were really true. But this it didn't matter to him as far as he was able to provide him an adequate answer.

He moved closer to the spirit to address him but as he was about to get a hold of him, he disappeared allowing him to grab the wind. He was surprised at this magic, he looked around to see where he was but didn't see him. He stepped back preparing himself for the unexpected but he was pulled out of this by something that hit his head from the tree

He looked around the ground to see what it was and discovered that it was a pinecone. Manofield held on to his head in pain and this seemed hilarious to the shaman who was now sitting comfortably on a tree branch away from Manofield's grasp. He was holding another pinecone in his hands and this annoyed Manofield to no end.

He breathed heavily and thought of ways in which he could make Ishtar suffer, but he knew there was little he could do to him, as he needed his help. He detested the fact that with all the power that he had, all he could do was sit in the forest and act like the father of all animals. He thought of what he would have accomplished for himself if he had all the powers that he held. Dropping his anger for once, he spoke to him.

"Tell me the purpose that girl, Melody has here?" he asked.

Ishtar stared at him with a straight face for a while and Manofield mistook it for being oblivious of who Melody was.

"You should know Melody, what she is?" he spoke again to confirm if the shaman actually knew what he was talking about.

Ishtar looked at him for a while and was not sure what caused the sudden interest that Manofield took for Melody, but knowing that whatever answer he would give would not be harmful he decided to simply be honest with him.

"The majestic white wolf is here to find a way to cleave her wolf side from her human side," he announced to Manofield. He paused to gauge his reaction and it was as he expected-dumbfounded but he knew if he told him the remaining part of his announcement, he would be more than shocked.

"That is impossible, right?" he asked hoping that the shaman would answer negatively.

"It is and I already told her how she can achieve this," Ishtar told him.

"Wait, I don't seem to understand," Manofield spoke calmly trying to clarify what could be wrong.

His heart was racing as he knew what this could mean for his plan, if the shaman were speaking the truth.

"You mean it is possible for us werewolves to separate our shifter side from our human side." he asked even though he knew the answer he was going to get from Ishtar.

"No process is permanent. The human part and the wolf part were fused in the process of becoming a werewolf and the process can be reversed." Ishtar said.

It was not just Manofield that was struck upon hearing this news, on hearing the new possibility that had just shown itself, he moved back to absorb it. He had heard so many things that had added additional weight to his already heavy burden. His head was swirling in a bid to contain the information and his brain was not so sure what to think at the moment.

Manofield's hopes had just been shattered by what the shaman said, and it was driving him crazy. He knew if that kind of information got leaked to other wolves, not just his pack it might mean the extinction of werewolves, making the alphas lose power and relevance. He wondered why one would want to separate from such glorious gift. The rare privilege of having vast power and tremendous agility. Then his mind thought of only one reason for Melody to want to change- the human lover; Blaine.

His mind wondered how one that was gifted such a rare species of werewolf wanted to do away with it. Manofield didn't know exactly what to think. He had to keep what he had learned secret and while he was at it, he must not raise suspicion in his pack so they won't question the sudden urgency in his mission.

"I cannot afford to lose my pack," Manofield told himself.

"Why would you do that?" he angrily asked Ishtar who was now on his feet in front of him. "Why would you endanger the werewolf kingdom by putting such possibility forward?" he asked him with his eyes showing fury.

Ishtar knew that the Alpha's reaction had more to it than met the eye and even though he knew what it could be, he decided not to bring it into the picture.

"I am a lover and protector of animals, plants and humans alike, why trap someone or something that does not want to be?" he posed a question of his own.

Ryan had just recovered from the shock of what he heard Ishtar declare and his confused thoughts had now been replaced by just one goal, and that goal was to stop Melody from doing something that would be an abomination. Something no wolf should ever do or think of.

"I will not allow this," he proclaimed. "This ends now." He uttered again.

In a flash, he left the scene without being noticed by Manofield. He began his search anew for Melody, making a silent vow that he would not stop searching for her until she was found. He began to look for all the caves that he knew the locations of that she could have found shelter in to avert the storm.

Melody held the sleeping Blaine in her arms when she heard sounds coming from around the cave. She first thought it was an illusion; a fragment of what she wanted but the footsteps sounded more real with every minute that passed. She went out to see who they might belong to and was a bit relieved that they were foresters who had set out to search for anyone who had been stranded by the storm.

It was a common practice for the foresters to do this as the second most common cause of death after an animal attack in Echo Cove was being stuck in one of the snowstorms. Blaine used to lead the parties but since he was nowhere to be found, another had filled in for him. Melody scented the air to be sure that none of them had evil intentions before going back to the cave where she let out a very loud howl.

The howl was very loud and it alarmed the foresters who rushed towards the direction of the sound. Melody had left the cave to hide in a place that would keep her presence discreet but keep them in her eye line. The five foresters rushed into the cave and were pleased to see Blaine even though his life was still hanging by a thread. They picked him up gently and in no time they motioned to where their truck was parked. When she saw that he was safely in their truck, she knew where her next visit would be- the hospital to check up on Zane and make sure that Blaine reached the hospital safely.

The howl made by Melody might have served its purpose but it had at the same time had created unwanted attention for her enemy. Ryan was very lucky to hear the howl, he might not have been able to recognize the paw prints but he knew for sure that the howl he heard was not made by any member of his pack. He raced through the woods so as to catch the white wolf in time before she changed direction.

The truck got to the hospital faster than Melody, as she had to be sure no one trailed her to the place. But as she got closer to the hospital with just a tree shielding her from been seen, a figure deterred her from moving out of hiding. She had wondered not long that the Brown Billy wolf had stopped to rest but she was wrong. Ryan was outside the hospital looking like a night watchman who had been warned of a robbery that would take place that night. When Ryan was very sure that no one suspected him, he entered the hospital.

Melody had not seen such a wide variety of species of wolves before, but she had the feeling that the brown wolves were extraordinarily adamant and stubborn. When she was sure that Ryan was out of sight, she shifted back to her human form dusting off all the leaves and dirt her body had attracted on her run throughout the forest. When she was sure that she was now looking good, she took a deep breath and with her head held high and her shoulders straight, she walked inside the hospital and not feeling the need to ask for directions as to where her family was, she began to wander around with the hope that she would get some clue. It was also her way of knowing the exact location that Ryan was.

Sandy's friend and her dad, after waiting for few hours to see if Zane regained consciousness, went back home promising to come check on the in the morning. They had no sooner left than her brother was rushed into the hospital, he was unconscious, and she could hear the nurses' talk about hypothermia and how he was lucky to have been able to avert that because the situation could have cost him his life.

She waited for another long minute in the waiting room before the nurse that called her earlier beckoned to her that her brother was awake. Feeling overjoyed, she ran inside the ward and gave him a hug not caring if his body was bruised or sore.

"Were you crying?" Blaine asked her sounding very weak.

"No, I was not, the weather is a bit…" she didn't finish her statement before she hugged him again.

When she had confirmed that he was feeling better, she started asking him a series of questions. And he answered them in the order she asked them. He also narrated his ordeal with the wolves and how one of them was protecting him and how others were acting in a strange way, acting more goal-oriented like humans. He also told her that he thought he saw Melody and that she was the one that saved him from dying under the icy river. As he was still speaking, the door opened gently and Zane limped in, he still had numerous bumps and bruises and his forehead was still wrapped with bandages.

"Speak of the devil, I was about to ask about how you were," Blaine spoke up as soon as Zane entered the room.

"I thought I had lost you," he said.

Blaine chuckled, "It will take a lot more than two wolves to bring me down," he said with pride.

They were still enjoying the family reunion when Aunt Marina entered, she was wearing a very big raincoat, and her hair had been packed under a shower cap. Although she smiled on seeing that the three of them were safe but her eyes showed that she had probably cried the entire way back to town. The bones around her eyes were not visible and her eyes looked exhausted.

"I am so happy we are all here," she said.

They all screamed with joy on seeing her, they hugged one another and shed little tears of joy.

"I came as fast as I could. The storm was more intense than forecasted and I could not get here any earlier," she explained.

"You came at the right time," Blaine corrected her and they both laughed softly at one another.

Unbeknownst to them, the creature that was listening to them and was about to show itself if not for a statement that was uttered by Marina.

"There is something I want to tell you about our visitor Melody," she declared her voice sounding more serious now; this made everybody sit up to hear what she had to say.

Melody stood by the door and was not sure if she was sad because Aunt Marina just referred to her as a visitor, or that they wanted to have a conversation about her without even caring where she was. But regardless of this, she decided to hear what she could have possibly discovered about her that she wanted to share.

"Melody is not who we think she is," Marina had started to speak when she was sure she had the undivided attention of the three people she was addressing.

"She is not who we thought she was...is," she said again and when asked to come clean with what she knew, she said without remorse that she was a liar.

This new discovery took a huge toll on everybody, as they were all silent trying to see if there could be a better way to process the information. Melody had ran out of the hospital upon having her secret laid bare in such a dramatic manner. She couldn't even look at anyone in the room right now, she just wanted to run and escape her troubles.

Blaine was quiet trying to process the information he just heard. He never knew his aunt to lie, but surely she must be mistaken right? He looked out through the window lost in thought and his eyes caught a yellow pair of eyes staring at him but when he looked again, they were gone and all that remained outside was total darkness.

12

It's been days since the incident occurred on the icy river and her worse fear had not only been realized but her secret was also uncovered. She had listened to Marina talk about her discovery of her true identity. With a heavy heart, she had taken a final glance at them without waiting to hear what the family had to say about it. She knew no human would be able to comprehend the fact that werewolves aren't just folktales that they were real, and one of them was living among them.

She had sat by the oak tree weeping all day about how her life turned out to be but after some time, she decided to move to a nearby cave and take shelter there. She would leave every day to watch over the family. The first day of her watch was the saddest; she could see the sadness and quietness that had befallen the whole house. None of them were talking to one another and they all seemed to have red eyes from constant weeping. The only thing that served, as a relief to her heart was that the Brown Billy Pack had not come to disturb them and she had not picked up on any of their scents coming near any of the family.

She had spent a lot of time just sitting in the cave thinking over her life and what she still needed to do with the time she had left on the earth. She had spent over three days there and most of the time she survived on scavenged food and also stolen dry clothes to protect herself from the frigid weather outside. On one snowy night in the cave, she sat with her back to the wall as she began to think what might have happened if she told them earlier who she really is, and the main purpose of her coming to the town. But as powerful as she was, she could not predict the emotions of humans as she might have been rejected with contempt.

After spending three lonely days in the cave, she decided to take a bold step to see the family. She cleaned herself with the water from the defrosted ice and she prepared herself to see all of the people who once took her in as part of their family.

When she got to the door, she took a long breath and listened to check if she could hear any voices coming from inside but the house was all silent and yet, she was sure that the grave-silent house had living beings inside it, three living human beings.

She first thought of opening the door with the key she had but gave it a second thought, as she was not sure what their reaction would be to this. She summoned the courage to knock. Nothing happened the first time she knocked so she gave it another try, this time louder than the previous one. Then, she heard movement from inside coming towards the door. She moved backward as the door creaked opened slowly with Zane holding on to it to block the entry of whoever it was.

When she saw that it was Zane that opened the door, her heart melted away as she saw the bruises and the stitches that were done during his stay in the hospital. She remembered the pain that he had to experience that day and how the rock had badly injured him making him lose a lot of blood. Zane also upon seeing her broke into tears and quickly hugged her. They stayed in each other's arms for some time and Zane's tears sent a cold shiver down Melody's body. She wasn't sure what to expect when they broke their embrace.

There were a lot of things that he had wanted to tell her but all he could do at the moment was to cry out all the emotions he had bottled up. During the time that she had been gone they all had anticipated her return, he had begun to do some research about her and the illness which had made her come to the town and had found out a handful of information about her and the creature that resided within.

Zane opened the door wide for her to come in as she walked slowly into the house and walked straight to the kitchen. Sandy was there writing something in her school book with a pen while she held a pencil with her mouth. She wasn't aware of her presence and Melody kept looking at her from the kitchen entrance. Holding her breath and awaiting her reaction.

"Zane," she called. "Who was at the door?" she asked him but when she didn't hear him reply she stood and that was when she saw her.

Melody was standing right in front of her and she was not sure of precisely what she wanted to do. She felt like hugging her and pouring her heart out, but she didn't move an inch from where she was. They both stood at a distance as water began to trickle down from their eyes. Marina must have heard the sound of people crying as she suddenly came out of the storeroom in the kitchen to see what was going on. Being a strong woman, she held back her tears but her eyes began to turn red and betray her turbulent emotions.

"Where have you been, Melody? We have been looking all over for you," she spoke.

Melody wiped her tears off as she at the same time cleared her throat before talking.

"I am so sorry for not coming earlier, I was making arrangements for my new accommodations." She spoke quietly with her voice breaking as she did. She paused for a moment to gather her thoughts before speaking again.

"I have been a trouble to you all long enough. You offered me shelter, you offered me food, and you gave me joy and happiness and all I could repay you with is hurt and pain. I don't want to do that anymore. I have to take my leave now and make it on my own." she stated.

She waited for them to say something but they all looked at her in astonishment and sadness. Seeing that none of them wanted to talk, she continued speaking.

"Now that I am leaving, I think it is high time I tell you some things about me. Although some of them I think you already know." she uttered, she was trying to be strong in order to tell them the things they might not know about her.

"My name is Melody Sophia and the Great Donovan is my uncle. I am a classically trained violinist but recently I had to leave my home and travel to this place as I was diagnosed with cancer for the second time. This was the town where I visited when I was young before my parents died so I came here to clear my headspace." she told them.

They all stood on the spot crying their eyes out as Melody told them the sad story of her family and why she had to come to the town. When she was done with what she had to say, Blaine came out from where he was. He had stood from the couch where he stayed hidden until he heard Melody's life story. She told them also that staying in the town brought her closer to her parents and also staying with them showed her the things she had not had in her life since her parents' death.

"I didn't mean to hurt any of you," she said in tears now as she looked at Blaine.

"I am just trying to live the rest of my days in peace and happiness and I am sorry for all the trouble that I might have caused you."

Unable to hold back the tears any longer, she ran upstairs to where her room was and shut the door behind her. She was surprised to see the different cards welcoming her back were used in decorating the room and aside from that, the room still looked exactly the same from the last time she saw it.

Melody began to pack her clothes putting them in her bags and the stream of tears plopped on the clothes she was packing. She sat down after some time when her heart could no longer bear the pain that was going on in her life. She laid on the bed and rolled in pain that seemed to be coming from all over her body. Her mind traveled to Blaine, how sad he looked when she saw him, the redness of his eyes and how quickly he had lost weight and it seemed like he had aged overnight.

"Is this how he would feel when I die, leaving him behind?" she asked herself then the thought of leaving him struck another blow to her heart again.

Sandy was still standing in the same spot even after Melody had ran up to her room. At first, they could hear movement from her room then it became all quiet again. Sandy had come to love Melody not just as a guest but as a sister and among the things that she had wanted to tell her was not to leave, but she couldn't find the words. She looked at Blaine who was just moving away from the kitchen and without getting to see his face she knew that he was not himself. He was known to always walk with his shoulders held up high and his gaze fixed to the front but at the moment, he slouched and his eyes were looking at the ground resembling a dejected man who had lost it all.

Zane hugged his mother who could no longer contain the tears that threatened to spill from her eyes. He had always seen her be a very strong lady who was healthy in every way possible but the news of her having cancer was a big shock for her. She also watched as Blaine moved out of the Kitchen.

"Sandy, Zane," she called out to the two of them as she made to follow Blaine out of the kitchen. "Make sure Melody stays in the house, no matter what. I will be right back, I need to speak with Blaine." She spoke authoritatively.

She quickly followed her nephew. Blaine had stopped to take a quick gaze at the stairs and when he had seen enough, he grabbed his coat from where he hung it and went out of the house. Marina also grabbed her jacket and then the car keys as she joined Blaine outside.

The breeze outside was gentle although it didn't hide the fact that it was still bitterly cold. Blaine had put on his coat but Marina had yet to do that.

"Blaine," she called her nephew quietly and she held on to his arms.

"I know this is hard for you but this is not the time to start over thinking or licking your wounds. We need to talk. So, you head on to town and pull up a stool at the local bar. Wait for me there, I will join you soon." She ordered Blaine giving him the keys to his car.

Blaine looked at his keys for few seconds before he nodded and began walking to where he parked and zoomed off. His head was aching and the pain he was feeling made him remember the day he lost his parents, how he felt when the officers came to his aunt's house to deliver the news. He thought of Melody and the little time that they have spent together whether alone or with the whole family, he could see the picture of her joyful smile in his head and then that picture would be suddenly replaced by the tears he saw in her eyes minutes ago.

Although he had lots of conflicting emotions, one thing he was sure of was that he loved Melody with every beat of his heart and would do anything to get her hand in marriage, but the thought of what would become of him when she died made any decision he planned on taking very hard.

Marina waited outside for Blaine's SUV to get out of sight before entering the house again. She headed straight for Melody's bedroom and gave it a light knock. Nobody answered but when she turned the knob of the door, it sprang open.

"Melody." she said upon seeing her frantically packing her things.

She had already most of her stuff packed and was about to begin taking two of her bags downstairs. On hearing her name, she stopped short frozen to the spot and started another round of tears. She had thought that her tear glands would have run dry but seeing Marina again made the tears come rushing back to her eyes. She started sobbing out loud and her anguished cries could be heard all the way downstairs by Zane and Sandy.

Marina entered the room but didn't close the door very well as it bounced open halfway when she left the doorway, she looked at her and the thought of losing her terrified her. Not able to bear not seeing her, they heard footsteps running up the stairs as Zane and Sandy came upstairs to join them and the three of them all gave her a group hug and they all started sobbing in unison. Melody had never felt love and acceptance like this before in her life, not even when she was with her uncle before he died. She was lost as she was suffering from a disease that was not possible for a werewolf to have and the way to combat it was not clear to her.

Even though she was dying gradually inside, she had never felt so alive and the only thing that was making her cry was the fact that she was going to leave the awesome family that made her feel so incredibly loved in the last few moments of her life. The thought of losing the love of her life compounded the things that made her cry and she wondered how her life would be so happy if she was not battling the deadly cancer that was already set on claiming her life.

When they broke apart she sat on the bed again and looked at the reflection in the mirror but instead of seeing herself, she was staring at the white wolf.

"I will set you free, my love," she soliloquized.

The majestic white wolf was a part of her and had helped her in immeasurable ways and the only thing she could do for it was to set it free from the bondage of her deteriorating self. Long before this moment, she had always thought herself to be a nobody to everyone and that her demise would not hurt or mean anything to others, but the recent happenings made her think otherwise.

Sandy was a bit amazed at the way Zane had broke down and was crying like a baby, he had always talked about being strong and could not shed tears for any reason, but when he realized that Melody, the fearless woman that helped him out weeks ago and also kept his secret would die soon. The thought of Blaine being heartbroken also sent shockwaves of fear, pain, and sadness to his heart. Sandy knew if Melody died, her brother might not be able to pick up the broken pieces of his heart and move on.

"I need to go to town now," Marina spoke. "I want to go and try and knock some sense into Blaine. We need to face this as a family."

She stood up as the three of them just stared at her. She

instructed Melody not to leave the house no matter what and when she made it back with Blaine they would all have a nice dinner like they have always done. She looked at Melody to see her reaction but all she did was sob

"None of this is your fault, you need to understand that, we don't hold anything against you. We are family," Marina reminded Melody and Melody nodded affirmatively in tears.

She made it out of the room and used the hem of her shirt to wipe off the tears before going back to her room to wash her face and then apply makeup to cover the gloomy and lean face of hers. She was quick with this and then she picked her car key then head for the driveway to get the car warmed up.

When she had pulled out of the driveway and was out of the compound, Sandy and Zane also stood up to leave Melody to rest.

"Melody, I love you...we all do," Zane spoke.

"I love you too. All of you," she replied to him in tears.

"Get some rest, we'll be right downstairs if you need anything." Sandy said as they closed the door behind them.

Melody could not believe the amount of love still shown by the family to her. It was as if none of them heard the fact that she was a werewolf. One of the things that she did when she discovered that she was a wolf was to check the series of movies and articles on how people might react if they know a werewolf is real. Most of the answers were wicked and inhumane and it was one of the reasons she stayed to herself without having friends or any form of close attachment, it also was the best way for her to hide her identity.

She laid properly on the bed and tried to concentrate in order for her to reach the wolf, for she was lost and wanted nothing than to hear it say something about what was going on with her. It was the wolf that had always stayed with her in times of trouble and had also been a very good adviser on most of the matters that she had presented to it. When she was able to become connected to the wolf part, the wolf was already waiting for her at the oak tree.

The weather at the oak tree was cool as it was neither cold nor warm. The place was filled with dark fog and the only thing that she could see from afar was the white wolf. For the first time since she had the wolf in her. It met her halfway before they both went back to the tree. The wolf sat in between her legs and it gave a sad whine. But before she could say anything to the wolf, she drifted into a deep slumber.

13

Melody had no sooner drifted into a deep slumber than she found herself again sitting next to the oak tree, wearing the long blue gown she always wore anytime she found herself in the trance. She also heard the growl of the white wolf at the other side of the tree and was pleased to see that it was still there watching over her. They didn't communicate for some time and Melody could decipher that the wolf was not happy with her decision. After sitting for a while without any communication Melody spoke to the white wolf.

"I have missed you," she said to the wolf and the wolf whom Melody understood without speaking replied that it didn't want her to carry on with the decision she had made.

It was the first time the wolf would be pleading to Melody. The wolf didn't want to leave Melody no matter what happened and it was ready to face the consequence of its actions. But no matter the reasons that it gave Melody, its protests fell on deaf ears. The wolf also persuaded her to stay with her family and that it was impossible for her to cut off all that love just because she was supposed to die very soon, and she didn't know what heaven might have in store for her.

"Heaven is dead," Melody spoke in annoyance. "They couldn't help me when I needed them... when we needed them." she stuttered.

The wolf, on the other hand, was doing all that it could to change Melody's decision and it was as if the atmosphere was following its mood as the wind stood still and dried leaves began to fall one at a time. As they continued with their argument, Ishtar was watching them from one of the high tree branches. He had yet to believe that Melody would do anything to set the wolf free even when the wolf didn't want to leave her.

He remembered the day she was brought to him many years ago and he appeared to them in a modern style hoping they would think he was too good to be true. He would never have thought that the once seemingly weak girl would grow up to be selfless and strong in the presence of danger that might even claim her life. She was exceptionally kind and her good heart had struck him as it had struck the majestic white wolf.

As he looked at Melody, a teardrop fell from his eyes, moving down to his cheek then it started falling. It touched a dry leaf and the leaf turned green immediately. Ishtar truly was all powerful but there was a limit given to his power and he could not go against the bidding of the gods and the gods had yet to make their decision known, but he was sure that they were touched by what was going on. How could they not be? He looked up to the sky and as if he saw one of the ancient gods, he bowed his head then gave a broad grin as if something new was made known to him.

The wolf rose to its feet and went to where Melody was sitting, it looked at her for a while and then started moving closer to her. It was a sign that it was not going to leave her no matter what. Melody hugged it once it reached her and whispered in its ear.

"I will not let you die, I promise," she said then pecked her.

Only one car parked in the driveway after about two hours since they left, it was Marina and Blaine. As they got out of their car, Marina went to where her nephew was and gave him a hug.

"You will be alright dear." she said to him.

His body was still oozing the smell of the numerous drinks that he ordered. It so happened that when Marina told him to wait for her at the local bar, he had decided to drown his sorrows by drinking, then one drink turned to two until he lost count and was nearly drunk. When Marina got to the local bar, she had seen him with a row of empty glasses in front of him but was not sure if her eyes deceived her, as she had never seen Blaine order any form of hard liquor. When asked by his other foresters why he was like that he would reply:

"I am a proud person, I cannot afford to be controlled by anybody much less something that is contained in a glass."

But seeing him that night brought another jolt of sadness into her heart, as she knew that he was at his breaking point. She went to him to check on him and when she got there and dragged him away gently from the table he was drinking at to another, he pulled out something from his pocket laughing hysterically.

"This is the ring I wanted to propose to Melody with," he said laughing out loud and drawing lots of attention to himself.

Everyone looked at him and were surprised seeing him drunk.

"I wanted to propose to her with this ring," he screamed out louder than before.

He took another drink from the tray the waitress brought him but his aunt quickly collected that glass from him and most of the drink poured on his lap. Marina knew he was heartbroken by what happened and he was not sure of how to process the whole thing. She knew the major reason for his reaction was that the love was true and it was also the first time that he would love that hard since his parents passed away.

"I am sorry Aunt Marina. I am really sorry." He apologized regrettably.

Marina consoled him telling him that it was not his fault and love just happened and that she also loved Melody but she had to keep it to herself because none of them could afford her to break down. They wept together and people around wondered what could be wrong with them. A man from nowhere came and offered them a white handkerchief each.

"I don't know what might have happened to you folks. But I am really sorry and I could not possibly imagine the pain you are going through," he said and walked away before any of them could see his face.

When Blaine looked back to see the man again he was nowhere to be found. It was Ishtar that came to them to console them in the little way that he could. He had been thinking of the family lately and for the first time in centuries, he was concerned and worried about humans. He had lost faith before in humans but what was unraveling before his very eyes was different and strange to him. He had known humans to be at their worst in situations like this but not this family. They were ready to go any length to prove their love to Melody and all Melody was doing was reacting with pure love and selfless attitude. Invisible to them, he touched the shoulder of Blaine and disappeared.

Marina and Blaine spoke about what their next line of action would be and Blaine said his mind was made up that he was going to help Melody no matter what and would go to any extent to find her a cure before it was too late.

"I cannot afford to lose her, Aunt Marina," he spoke. "I don't know how my life will turn out without her."

He later explained what he had been keeping quiet about since the incident on the ice to Marina. He told her that he was sure that he saw Melody doing her best to save him when he fell into the icy river and was able to catch a glimpse of her before he blacked out. His aunt looked at him in amazement and surprise about this and to further his point, he narrated his dream of him marrying Melody just before some brown wolves came to disrupt the ceremony. When they had all spoken their heart, they left the bar with lots of gazes escorting them out.

They both hung their jacket at the coat stand located by the door and Sandy rushed to the sitting room to welcome them. They had all stopped crying but their eyes were still red and their voice clogged with emotion. Blaine didn't sit down instead he was headed upstairs where Melody's room was but as he moved past Zane, his way was obstructed.

"Where are you going?" Zane asked, his voice sounding much clearer than when he greeted them.

"I am going upstairs to see Melody," Blaine replied to Zane with his eyes fixed on the stairs.

Zane objected to this as he told him that she was asleep and that it would be better if she was to be left alone. Blaine stood still for a while to think about it and deep inside he knew that he was also feeling exhausted emotionally and physically and it would be best if they didn't see each other for now. They both went back to the sitting room and they turned on the TV as they watched in silence. Zane's head was rested on his mother's shoulders and Sandy placed her head on Blaine's lap. The calmness was soothing their spirit as they were feeling recharged staying together and knowing that they would do anything for their sick family member.

After about thirty minutes, they had all dozed off and the remote for the television had dropped from Zane's hand. All of them didn't have any idea what evil await them just outside the house. The Brown Billy Wolf Pack had been watching the family for some time, and they were waiting for all of them to be inactive before they launched their attack , as they believed it would mean less collateral damage. When they were sure that all of them were asleep and coincidentally, the moon was at its brightest that night that's when they would strike.

Manofield in his wolf form walked out of the bush that he had stayed concealed in and behind him were six wolves; Kris, Ryan, Sage and three other wolves from the grey wolf pack. They were once an ally to Manofield but their thirst for power had made Manofield chase them out of the city threatening them that if they ever come back, he would kill them.

Manofield after hearing about the real mission that brought Melody to town had swallowed his pride and went to the nearest town which was where the gray wolves made their home. He informed Marius, the alpha of the pack of the impending danger that he had discovered. And although they didn't see eye to eye on so many things, they all concluded that it was really a threat. Marius instead of coming himself sent three of his strongest pack members along for back up. On getting close to the house, he growled an order, telling them to surround the house allowing no room for escape.

It was this growl that Blaine heard and even though the first thought that he was suffering from his own imagination, Zane, Marina, and Sandy jolted up as well.

"What was that?" Zane asked sounding scared.

Blaine moved to the nearest window and gently pulled the curtain aside to see what was outside. He saw about three brown wolves outside and they all resembled the ones that attacked him and Zane days ago.

"What do they want?" he asked himself in frustration.

He turned to his family and not wanting to strike fear into his heart smiled a bit then spoke to them.

"We have some wolves lingering outside." he said but before any of them could comment he continued with what he had to say. "But don't be scared. Just go upstairs; I will deal with this in no time. No matter what happens, don't make a sound and do not come out until I come get you." he ordered them.

He picked up his phone to call for help but there was no reception, so he instructed Zane and Sandy to try to call for help with their phones when they got upstairs. He went straight to his room to get the gun that he would use to scare them off. Blaine was oblivious of so many things that were happening outside the house as the first thought that they were only three wolves not knowing that four of them were still lurking around the house, and also that the wolves just so happened to wander up, he didn't believe that there was anything like werewolves in real life, despite what his aunt thought.

When he got to his room, he saw that there were wolves at that side of the house as well and then he realized that the count had just reached seven wolves in total that surrounded the house.

"Bastards, it's the whole pack," he murmured to himself as he took out his gun and lots of ammo. .

When they got upstairs, Melody was already awake. In fact, she was the first to notice the wolves presence and through their heartbeat and smell, she discovered that there were seven circling the house. She knew that since the Billy wolves knew that could not overpower her alone, they would ask for reinforcements from a local pack. She closed her eyes to communicate with the wolf and on seeing the wolf by the oak tree she breathed a sigh of relief, it was standing ready to take charge of the fight as they both knew that was the only way for them to stay alive and protect their family.

She noticed that it was raining in her trance but it was not just ordinary rain as it was red as blood itself. She didn't know what it meant but speculated that it might mean a bloodbath was imminent. The wolf began to move closer to her when they were facing each other it looked up to acknowledge the presence of Ishtar. Melody also raised her eyes upward and she saw Ishtar descending down to the ground.

He looked in the direction of Blaine's house from the oak tree then he spoke.

"It's time to wake up child, you have unwanted guests." he said.

His words and the noise made by rushing footsteps entering her room woke her from her trance.

"What is wrong?" she asked them trying to look confused.

None of them replied as Zane opened the curtain of her large window and there, she saw seven wolves. She looked around to see if everyone was in the room but realized that one person was missing.

"Where is Blaine?" she asked them.

"He is downstairs, he wants to see if he could scare them away with his gun," Marina replied looking out the window.

But Melody knew that he would need more than a gun to scare them away. He was making the same mistake everyone she had ever seen in movies make, thinking that the arrival of the wolves was just coincidence.

"He might not be able to do that all by himself," she soliloquized.

Marina asked what she said but fibbed about it. After contemplating for a while she could feel the majestic white wolf wanting to come out and deal the other wolves so she excused herself from the room telling them she would want to help Blaine. Before anyone could object to this, she rushed out and shut the door behind her. Zane and Sandy had been trying to place calls but it was as if the service line to the cell tower had been cut off because none of them could make a call.

Blaine had picked a strategic location in the house where he would find it easy to shoot the wolves outside and at the same time get a clear shot at anything that wanted to breach the door. He heard a sound from the porch and suddenly the door burst open. Surprisingly to him, he saw a lanky man with very broad shoulders walk inside, holding a cane that had a gold wolf head. Blaine didn't care if he was human; he didn't know him and was an unwanted guest at the time so he aimed the gun at the intruder's chest.

"Who are you?" he asked him holding the gun tightly against the man.

Manofield looked at him with a belittling eye, gave a grin before speaking.

"Child, I applaud your bravery but all I am here to do is to offer you a most generous exchange." He uttered waiting for Blaine to process what he had said.

"What the hell do you mean by exchange?" he asked angrily making the last word show all the contempt he could muster.

"Give Melody to me and we will leave your family alone. It's that simple." He stated his offer.

"Are you nuts? Who do you think you are to make such a demand? Don't you see that wolves are outside the house?" He fired back.

"Let me give you a piece of advice, Captain Obvious," Blaine replied, as he no longer enjoyed the conversation.

"You are not welcome here, I suggest you leave this house now. You have a better chance to survive with the wolves than here, my gun will make sure of that." he threatened him.

"Now, now. Is that a threat?" Manofield asked, now laughing at the amount of ignorance of Blaine showed.

He turned back as if he wanted to leave but instead made some funny sounds and one of the wolves began to come closer to him. He smiled cruelly as he turned to Blaine again.

"You were saying?" he asked tauntingly.

The wolf was Ryan and he was quite bloodthirsty at the moment. Blaine was surprised to see that the wolf was listening to Manofield and this made him even more frightened so in annoyance, he squeezed the trigger while the gun still aimed at Manofield.

The bullet was dispersed from the barrel fast but just as it was about to hit Manofield, he dodged it with just a broken button to show for the shot. He realized that he must have underestimated Blaine and his shot was on target and might not be able to dodge all the bullets he had.

"A true forester," he thought to himself "it's a shame you will have to die."

He looked at the awaiting wolf and then at Blaine. He pointed at Blaine and the wolf understood what he meant and charged towards him, running with top speed. His teeth were out as he ran. Blaine was trying to reload before the wolf could reach him but Melody who had been watching them knew it was impossible for him to get a shot at Ryan, even if he was able to reload in time so she came rushing down the stairwell screaming at him to duck.

He reacted to this fast enough for Melody to be able to launch herself over him. When he rose to see where Melody landed, he didn't see her at all instead he saw a beautiful white wolf bearing a close resemblance to the one from his dream. The white wolf had moved against the brown wolf and met it midway in the air crashing it into a table. The brown wolf yelped in pain as its side was already bleeding.

The white wolf, on the other hand, landed on its feet and made a threatening growl at Manofield. Blaine noticed that there was something odd about the guy as he was neither moved nor afraid of the wolf even though he kept his distance.

On hearing the gunfire and the crash, Kris and Sage rushed inside to see what was happening. On seeing that Ryan was down, they had wanted to attack the white wolf but Manofield ordered them not to as the fight was his.

One of the grey wolves had snuck in through the back of the house and having seen the opportunity, he moved to attack Blaine. As he got close to him and was about to bite his leg, Kris gave a counter-attack, pushing his body against the grey wolf and making it lose its balance. Blaine was surprised by the turn of events, but when he looked at the wolf closely he recognized it to be the brown wolf he helped days ago.

His mind quickly drifted back to that time and he still wondered if Melody was there or if it was just an illusion. He knew someone had saved him before he blacked out but all he saw was Melody and then a white wolf.

Could the white wolf be Melody? he thought to himself, surprised that he had not thought of that possibility before.

When Manofield had seen enough of all that had happened, he set his cane aside and then slowly, his huge body was bent and his fingernails turned into claws, he kept transforming right before Blaine's eyes till all was left was a very large brown wolf whose tail was long and its eyes were red as opposed to the bright topaz of the others. It was no doubt that he was the alpha wolf.

His pack members, Kris inclusive gave a bow as their alpha took its full wolf form. He would have loved nothing more than to teach Melody a lesson, the kind of lesson that would break her forever but he wanted her to marry him. He concluded that he was going to hurt her but won't kill her and all he wanted to do was to pass a message across to all that were looking- Manofield is the Alpha of all Alphas.

Sage was already beside Ryan and was tending to his wound by licking it with her tongue. She didn't want to transform into a human as her help might be needed in the fight any time. All attention was drawn to the battle that was about to happen between the majestic white wolf and the most ruthless Alpha of all time. When Blaine realized that his attention was diverted, he took the opportunity to target Manofield. The gun followed him to where he was going so when he dashed towards Melody he took a clear shot to his leg. The shot was unexpected and it struck fear in every one of them. Seeing that their leader had been injured, Kris and the grey wolf he attacked earlier ran out through the back door while Sage helped Ryan escape. Manofield, on the other hand, changed direction as he crashed through the window in pain to escape further injury and even worse; death.

Knowing that he had been wounded, she allowed him to escape. She turned back to see if any of the wolves were still there but they had all retreated. She walked outside and could still see that the wolves were all waiting for her outside. She transformed into her human self and moved closer to them without fear.

"This is my family. If you hurt even a strand of hair on their head, I will find you all and I will kill you," she warned them.

On hearing this, they all fled with their tail tucked between their legs.

She turned back to the white wolf and gave a very loud howl that could be heard miles away. She later entered the house and shut the door behind her in her wolf form. Exhausted by what had just happened, she fell to the floor with her head hitting the floor hard and then she shifted back to a human again, as Blaine moved closer to her, he saw a trail of blood flowing down her cheek.

14

———————

It had been two days since the violent attack of the Chorus's house. Although the house had been cleaned up to look as good as new, the scars inflicted by the werewolves still lingered in the mind of all the occupants. Melody had been unconscious for the most part of the two days spent at the hospital and unlike the times that she had spent in the hospital before then, she was hovering near death. And even though she wanted to communicate with the wolf, she was too weak to take the astral journey to the oak tree.

The afternoon sun was shining bright, working to absorb the water from the rain that fell the previous night but people around Echo Cove didn't seem to mind. Blaine was one of the rare people that still believed so much in the weather updates in the morning news regardless of how inaccurate they might have been in past times. On getting to the hospital with a large collection of fragrant flowers-he headed straight to the ward that housed Melody. He spotted the doctor heading out to another floor of the hospital so he hurried towards him to get an update on her condition.

"Hello doctor," he called to him

The doctor exchanged pleasantries with him, the doctor knew the reason he had stopped him so he saved him the stress of asking about Melody's condition, as he was also running on a tight schedule.

"Blaine, you are my good friend, you know that?" the doctor started to talk.

Blaine was not sure why he had asked such a redundant question, but he knew it was to prepare him for what he wanted to say next, so he nodded in affirmation. The doctor smiled at him as he continued to talk.

"I have good news and then bad news in regards to your girl-friend," he said.

He didn't know precisely how to react to this but met the doctor's sympathetic gaze head on.

"Let's get the bad news out of the way first, shall we?" he inquired but without waiting for a reply, he continued on. "Melody's case is getting worse by day. She keeps getting weaker and weaker and there is nothing that we can do for her now except to keep her comfort-able." he said and he knew that it got to Blaine as his eyes were turning red and the frown lines on his forehead were becoming more visible.

"But the good news is this, she is awake, she can speak with you and you can spend some time together." he informed him and he moved on without waiting for him to say anything.

By the time Blaine had processed all that the doctor had said, he had no one to talk about it with. So, he only held on to two things-that the doctor referred to Melody as his girlfriend and that she was awake after about two days of being unconscious.

He composed himself as he moved inside the ward. From what he had heard of werewolves, he knew that it was possible she heard all that was discussed by the doctor. On stepping inside her room, Melody tried to sit up and was helped by Blaine.

She was now looking paler than before and her hair had started falling out. Even though her face was white and cold, her beauty still remained the same and her eyes still held the charisma that they always had but now only with immense sadness reflected in their depths.

"Hi, girlfriend," Blaine greeted her when she was comfortably resting back against her pillows with the head of the bed elevated.

She tried to object to that but he gave her a hush sign by raising his index finger to her lips. Blaine sat by her bed and held on to her hand. They kept looking at each other and momentarily one of them would smile then they would act as if they wanted to cry before the cycle started over again.

"How is everybody?" Melody finally broke the silence that had descended on them. .

She was finding it quite hard to speak as her breathing had been labored since she woke up. But even with that, her voice still was as melodic as her name suggested. Just as it was the first day that Blaine heard her speak.

"They are fine. We are all staying at a nearby motel now." he answered her.

She asked if they have been disturbed by the wolves anymore since the incident, but he replied that they haven't and that all the foresters and hunters had been sent to hunt them down. She was relieved that the family was saved but at the same time worried that those that sought the wolves might be biting off more than they bargained for.

After another moment of long silence had passed, he told her about how the police were also taking up the issue and they have all told them all they knew about the attack. Granted, they omitted the fact that the wolves were actually werewolves and that Melody was also one of them even though she was completely innocent. .

Melody in her heart knew that there was nothing that would stop Manofield from launching new attacks on her and the family, and there was only one solution she could think of... which was letting go of the white wolf and waiting for her death alone.

On the other side of the hospital where the doctor was rushing off to laid a man who was as badly hurt as Melody, it was his ankle that was twisted badly and he refused to tell anyone how the injury came about.

Ryan had intentionally twisted his ankle so he would be admitted to a room close to where Melody would be so he could spy on her and get to know more about her and what she planned on doing. And unlike Melody, the doctor was happy that he was improving with the drugs that they prescribed for him.

Blaine presented her with the bouquet that he had handpicked for her and she really appreciated him for trying to inject her drab hospital room with some vibrant color.

"You are not scared this is Wolfsbane?" she teased.

They both laughed at this before Blaine asked if what he saw that day was true. Melody did not know how to come clean to him on that so all she did was nod in affirmation. Another dead silence came between them. Blaine, if asked about werewolves a few days ago, would have laughed it off as a crazy joke and nothing but a fictional tale for movie lovers, but what he had seen was a confirmation of realms that humans know nothing about. Melody knew it was time to be honest with him since they were clearly in love with each other and she was dying, so she had nothing to lose telling him everything about her- everything about who and what she is.

"Blaine, I love you." she uttered with every ounce of conviction she possessed.

Blaine looked at her shocked, as he was caught off guard by her plain confession of her feelings. He used his fingers to wipe off the tears that were flowing down her cheek.

"I love you too," Blaine replied tenderly.

"I have something else to tell you," she continued.

"What is that Melody?" he asked quizzically.

"I love you so much and I have never loved anyone as I have loved you. I was wandering in the darkness before I met you and you brought so much life into my world. You melted away my sadness and created a new world of family love and happiness for me, something I never thought was possible in my life."

Blaine looked at her with love as he also felt the same thing for her and everything was going wrong in his life before he met her, and since that time, she had brought so much joy and happiness not just to him but to his entire family. He tried to cut in but Melody beat him to it.

"Remember I told you this was not my first time here?" she asked him and he nodded.

"The first time I was here, I was brought by my family to find a cure for my cancer."

She continued to relay the story of how she was cured of cancer after meeting with Ishtar, who had told her parents to leave her alone in a cabin in the middle of the forest the night of the blue moon. She explained how the bite from the white wolf cured her and only to find out that the wild beast had not just bitten her but had done something more.

Ryan had wanted to enter to wreak havoc on the two of them as he had planned and was ordered to do but her story captivated him into waiting to hear how it all ended before he could decide what to do with her.

Melody went on describing how she bonded with the white wolf, who had allowed her to live an extra sixteen years even though she had lived it swimming in guilt and regret of what she did to her parents. But now that she was dying, she needed to let go of the wolf so it would not die with her and it was the main reason why she had come to town-- to save the wolf and its species from going extinct.

"Have you seen Ishtar?" Blaine asked her surprised.

She looked away from him. Her mind went to the time she saw the shaman and thought that the answer she would get would be something very easy. But the condition was as tough as letting the wolf go. She was lost in thought until Blaine touched her shoulder.

"Melody, what did Ishtar say the solution is?" he asked her again knowing that she was hiding something from him.

Melody looked at him and fresh tears spilled from her eyes. Blaine could not stand the tears, he hugged her tight and as much as he wanted to stroke her hair he didn't so instead, he rubbed her back gently. He thought of how painful the process of changing to a were-wolf must be. They broke apart when she was able to get her tears under control. But she was not saying anything about what Ishtar might have told her to do to set the wolf free.

"The shaman," she started talking. "Gave me an option, the only option really… to release the wolf from my body. I have just two days left before I can save the wolf and I am willing to do anything to save the wolf and the only thing that can save the wolf is my love. I need love to set it free." She spoke incoherently.

Blaine sighed on hearing this and held her by her shoulders and looked straight into her eyes.

"You are the most important person in my life. You are the best thing that has ever happened to me. I love you and I don't think I can love anyone as I have for you again in my life." Blaine also professed his undying love for her.

"I will do anything to help you fulfill your wish Melody, but you have to promise me one thing," Blaine said.

Melody looked at him through her tears, as she would never have thought that he would accept to do that as fast as he did. So she decided to ask what his condition was.

"What is that?" Melody asked in a sotto voce.

"You will have to promise me that you will stay with me for the rest of the time you spend on earth." he stated tenderly.

Melody began to weep like a baby as she heard this; she nodded her head in agreement to this. Blaine hugged her tight and she did the same. Melody was indescribably happy at this but at the same time, she was also sad about it. She had always experienced sadness in her life and she had caught an all too brief glimpse of happiness since she met Blaine's family, but what she was feeling right now was different.

She was very happy and yet sad, her tears were those of sadness, and yet they also expressed happiness from the bottom of her heart.

"I have always known that I would end up loving someone different," Blaine whispered to her.

"The same for me too," Melody answered him in a whisper before they let go of each other.

Melody's weakness and emotions had blocked most of her wolf

side as she, on a normal day would have noticed the presence of someone like her lurking around the hospital. Ryan heard all their conversation and was quite surprised at the two of them. He got to see things that he never thought possible and he heard the things he only would have seen in a fairy tale and yet it was real, unfolding just a few inches away from him.

He was moved by what he just witnessed. Unknowingly, tears began to fall from his eyes. He only knew the white wolf and not Melody. He had hated her since the day she saved the driver and his passengers, but when she told him that she was there for a different reason other than attacking his pack and she had a mission of her own, he had thought it was a lie to usurp them from the town.

His mind went to the folktales about the legendary white wolf, of how aggressive and yet powerful it was. And that might be the main reason the white wolf had used her body as an abode even after curing her. The act of selflessness and kindness that was shown by Melody and Blaine made him have a change of heart.

He was not the type that would change his mind easily but the forces that surrounded this couple was just too powerful and too pure for him not to succumb to. As he thought of the things that Melody would have to do to save the white wolf, his mind went back to the main reason they were both at the hospital.

"Manofield," he thought and a sudden rage flowed through his veins and the need to protect Melody and Blaine overwhelmed him.

He knew nothing would change his mind as he was going to do whatever it takes to get what he wanted, and Manofield didn't care who or what would have to suffer for him to get it. Right then, he made a vow to make sure that Melody achieved her goal, even if keeping that vow made him have to go against the order from the pack and even Manofield himself. Although he realized that he might not be able to take on Manofield alone but it so happened that he was still wounded, as the bullet shot by Blaine was no ordinary one, it was from the bullets blessed under the full moon by the shaman himself.

"He is weak," he thought to himself.

He also thought of telling the other pack members, while he was not sure if they would be willing to protect the white wolf, by all means he was obligated to tell them. He would tell them of the true and pure intent of her goals and if they didn't believe they would cross that bridge when they came to it. Another thing struck his mind and it was the fact that Ishtar himself blessed her. Ryan was a ruthless werewolf but he had a strong faith in spiritual things.

He quickly removed all the bandages and monitors that were on his body as he walked out of the hospital dodging the CCTV and anybody that might recognize him. He only had one thing to do now, tell Manofield to call off the vendetta or face the consequences of doing otherwise.

15

____

Ryan was still surprised at the way things went at the hospital, he was just as surprised as he was when he first heard it. When he got to the cave he was very pleased to see that Kris and Sage were still there. He had feared that they might be part of those suspected in town for the attack even though they might not have concrete proof of that.

On getting to the cave Kris and Sage were so curious to hear the report even before Manofield heard about it. Ryan had second thoughts about telling them as they might think he was running from the fight, and worst of all report him to Manofield and treason or fear was not what he could condone.

"Ryan," Kris called him as he sat beside him by the fire.

Ryan looked deep in thought and yet he was not doing anything when he heard Kris call him, all he did was look at him as he took a cup of coffee from the boiling pot. Sage joined them too but didn't say anything. She had known Ryan for a long time and she knew he was a person of strong conviction and wouldn't talk unless he wanted to, so she decided to out-wait him.

After a long hour of sitting in silence, he looked at his two colleagues then gave a soft sigh. Kris wanted to question him on what happened at the hospital but he was gestured to by Sage to refrain from doing that.

"We need to stop the attack on the white wolf," he finally said in a very low voice, as he didn't want his words to be overheard by just anyone.

Kris and Sage looked at him as if he was mad and he didn't blame them. If he were to be in their shoes he was going to think he was mad and probably would have beat some sense into himself. But here he was doing what he had not thought possible.

"Why do you say that? Have you also been bewitched by the beauty of the white wolf?" Sage asked in contempt even though she knew that could not be the reason.

"No, that is far from it, there's something that we all don't know," he answered her.

"Then what is it?" Kris asked, quickly losing his patience.

"Do you know she's sick, the woman that shifts into the white wolf?" he asked them.

Sage quickly got to her feet then walked to where Ryan was and whispered to him that they knew and it was the reason they didn't kill her the time they had an encounter with her and it didn't matter. Ryan was amazed that they had known all along and yet hid that fact from him. He was now feeling a funny movement in his stomach and he took it as a warning, but he was not sure if it was to caution him from telling them or the danger that he was going to put them in by telling them.

"Whatever you have to say, you need to be fast about it. Remember that Manofield had pronounced our judgment." Kris reminded him.

It was after the raid into Blaine's house when Kris saved him from being attacked by the grey wolf. According to the wolf culture, it was a public humiliation and was punishable by death. Because of countless pleading from Sage, he was pardoned and instead of being killed, Manofield had told them to leave town before the red moon or they would be destroyed.

"Manofield is getting out of hand," Kris commented.

"He felt he has no use for us again and didn't want us to share in his glory," Sage corrected.

Ryan nodded at this, as it was true that Manofield would not have done that if he didn't have another plan. All along, he had secretly turned five humans into werewolves and they have all sworn to do his bidding no questions asked.

It was this that gave Ryan the confidence to tell them what he had heard from Melody. Like him, they pitied her and were also ready to stop what Manofield had planned for her. They felt the presence of another wolf coming and they quickly made a plan to meet at the diner where Blaine was known to come every day so that they could all formulate a plan. . Kris and Sage passed the secret opening out of the cave just in time to avoid being sighted by Manofield.

"What are you staring at?" Manofield asked Ryan who was trying to act normal and as if nothing had happened.

"Nothing." He replied I him. "I brought news for you from the hospital," he quickly said in order to change the subject.

"Yes, what is it," Manofield asked him hurriedly.

During his time of self-reflection, he had thought of so many things and he knew that for Melody to succeed, there must be an inside man who would know every aspect of Manofield's plan and he had to win his already fading trust for him back. So he told him about Melody's plan to go to the Asher Temple which was located about five miles away from the oak tree. The temple was built to face the oak tree directly and it was said that the temple was built from the tree where the seed for the oak tree was taken.

"Ryan," Manofield said. "I need you more than ever now. You have always been my right hand man. You are my most trusted friend."

Ryan was surprised to hear this from him as the many years that he had spent with Manofield, he had never appreciated all his efforts or anything he did.

"Why are you saying this now?" he asked him looking over at him, as he didn't believe his ears.

"Because it needed to be said," Manofield said, now rubbing his forehead against Ryan's own.

Manofield filled Ryan in on all that he had planned without being suspicious of him in the slightest, he even told him of the new members of the pack and how he planned to kill Kris and Sage when he was done with the mission at hand. When they were done with the conversation, Ryan told him that he was going to town to do some recon so the plan would go off without a hitch.

Manofield thanked him again for the support and also promised him with great gifts of power when they succeeded. Ryan pretended to be moved by this but his plan was totally different from his. When he got out of the cave, he made sure that no one was following him, which was why he had to travel the longest way possible through the forest to the diner.

Sage and Kris had barely taken their seat near where they used to see Blaine and they discussed the things that Manofield told him he wanted to do. Sage gasped at the horror and extent to which he was willing to go just to get what he wanted. Even though their plan was yet to be well polished, they wanted to tell Blaine of it as soon as possible so he could contribute and know that they were no longer a threat to him or his family.

When they had waited for an hour and didn't see Blaine, they made up their mind that their plan had to be carried out by them alone. Kris listened to the way Ryan was talking and trying to make sure that their plan worked and everyone's safety was taken seriously and he had a sudden likeness for him.

Before then, he never much liked Ryan, he saw him as a brutal and heartless member of the pack, however, what he was doing now was a complete deviation from who he knew.

"Ryan, I am sorry for all the times that I have hated you. I trust you and I am proud to stand with you no matter what." Kris said to him.

This caught Sage off guard, she knew all along that Kris never liked Ryan and all he had for him was fear, she would never have thought that he would confess that. The reason for the love lost among them was not farfetched.

They were the only two in the pack before and just one alpha. It was going well with them as the two were known for their bond and brutal ways of carrying out the orders given by their leader. Sage would snap a child's neck without remorse and bathe herself in the blood of a baby in front of its mother and still go to bed without being pricked by her conscience.

During a full moon in the summer, they had gone for a raid in the nearest town and when they were causing everyone to run for their life, Sage saw a boy who was totally fearless, even though wounded. This act of bravery moved Sage and since then she had kept him close to her and against Ryan's wishes, he was turned.

As if that was not the end since she took in Kris, Sage had been acting all motherly and Kris was the cause of their first fight, a fight they never truly recovered from. Ryan blamed Kris for letting her lose the killer instinct that she always had and because of Manofield's need to have more pack members they didn't kill or turn Kris away and it only served to vex Ryan more.

"So what are we going to do now?" Sage asked to break the silence.

"We will go to the temple and guard Blaine and Melody until everything they have to do is done and we will pray that the mother wolf will protect us all, during and after the fight," Ryan said.

Ryan told them that all they had to do was to buy them some time, but for this part of the plan to work they must be inside the temple right as the comet passed over. Ryan being well versed in the ancient history knew the significance of the comet for the wolf.

He also confessed that the mission might cost them their lives, but also explained that doing this will let them have the favor of the mother wolf when they die, as they would be known forever as the saviors of the last majestic white wolf.

He also warned the two of them to stay as far away from Manofield's reach or smell as possible as he had plans to kill them after the mission, something he could change his mind on if he caught a glimpse of them.

As they were talking, an old forester came to them and started pointing fingers at them that they were wolves but those inside the diner laughed him off as being mad. The three of them stood up in order not to draw attention to themselves and they all wondered where the old man got the idea from. While the old man was unknown to Ryan and Sage, the old man looked like someone he knew from his former town. He had thought that he died but regardless he was very happy that they got away from him before the scene he was trying to create got larger.

They stood in front of the diner for few minutes to discuss the next time they would meet before departing. Ryan instead of returning to the cave went to the oak tree to seek its blessing and probably to ask forgiveness for all that he had done in frustrating Melody's plan, a plan he believed to be divine.

When he was about to leave the oak tree, Ishtar granted him the honor of seeing him. He emerged out of the tree slowly. He had a large fur that resembled that of a grizzly bear draped around his body, he walked slowly to the front of Ryan with the shell of a tortoise in his hand. On reaching Ryan, he dipped his hands into the shell, wetting his hand with the moist red dust in it and used it to mark Ryan's forehead down to his cheek. Before Ryan could talk, the shaman disappeared and the only thing that remained was a gush of wind that seemed to talk to Ryan, saying.

"May the mother wolf bless you in your mission."

16

—————

It was D-day. The snow had covered all the ground and the valley was glistening white with everything looking calm and peaceful. The birds were in their nest and everywhere was quiet which made the sound of air beating against the trees sound like a noise. Melody was discharged the day that Blaine went to visit her as the doctor believed that what she needed was love and not further treatment as her health had declined so much there was nothing more medically they could do to extend her life.

When she was leaving the hospital, the nurses who had had the chance to speak with her or hear her story felt sad for her. They wept silently as they watched from corners unseen to her in sadness. She had reached a point in her life that she could no longer care for herself or feel pity for her state again, all that mattered was to make the most of the few days that she had left to live on earth to set the wolf free and she only had one chance at it.

On getting home that day, Marina had gone ahead of them in preparing the house for her arrival and she had also prepared her favorite meal to commemorate her return. She could not sleep that night, as she was scared of what would haunt her in her sleep.

She stared at the ceiling of her room lost in thought of what she had to do. She thought about the Brown Billy wolves and hoped they don't disturb her from achieving her goal. When it was morning, and the first light could be seen, it was then that her eyes got weary, she drifted slowly into a deep slumber but instead of having a calm sleep, she found herself at the oak tree.

She was sitting in the same spot that she always sat at the oak tree, she waited for the wolf to make a sound to declare its presence, but it didn't. She stood up to check what was wrong and there, the wolf was. She tried to touch it but could not no matter how hard she tried. Her hand would pass through empty air, as the wolf was not there.

She didn't know what was wrong and she screamed for the presence of Ishtar. The shaman didn't want to answer at first as he didn't like to come to her in her dreams, but it was a special situation so he decided to appear to her.

When Melody saw him, she quickly rushed to him telling him what was happening with her and the wolf. The shaman was not surprised by this and he motioned to another tree that faced where the wolf was sitting oblivious of their presence.

"My child, you are dying and the wolf is weakened too," he said.

"It's as if the wolf is not there yet I can see it." Melody lamented.

Ishtar explained to her that since her battle with the werewolves where she got very weakened, the wolf had to sacrifice some of its strength to keep her alive and the price it had to pay was to lose some form of connection with her. So instead of it being invisible to Melody. She will get to see it but it won't be able to feel her presence.

On hearing this, she wept profusely in her dreams.

"Why would the wolf do that?" she grieved.

"No matter what you want to do, Melody, the wolf loves you and would do anything for you. The two of you have the same love for each other and since that is the same thing you will do for it, the wolf didn't see anything wrong in doing it for you," Ishtar explained to her.

She gathered the courage needed to comfort herself as she knew the time for crying was over and the time for action was at hand. She talked to Ishtar on the fears that she had in regards of what she wanted to do, as the Brown Billy wolves were hell bent on causing harm to her family and her. Ishtar looked at her, as she didn't know what was going on at the other side. He had wanted to tell her but it wouldn't change anything so instead, he gave her a riddle.

"The unthinkable will be thought and the comet shall light the path of people's darkness while leaving some in it," the shaman said cryptically.

Melody didn't understand what this meant as she thought Ishtar was referring to her death and the freedom of the wolf, not knowing that it was not a riddle talking about her or any of her family.

When all the questions asked by her had been answered, the white wolf stood up all of a sudden and gave a loud howl. Melody wanted to try her luck to see if she could get her to see her but as she moved closer to it, everything around her went dark. She turned around to see where it went but she didn't. This made her scream out loud and all of a sudden, a blinding light shone on her.

She opened her eyes scared to the bone. She was back in her room and Blaine was sitting beside her and the light was from the sun as the curtain had been pulled away. She hugged Blaine tight as she was still shivering.

"You are alright now. It was just a dream. You are safe with me." Blaine consoled her.

Slowly her mind was calmed. Blaine looked at her then lay beside her to help her rest assured that she was safe. After some time, they stood up from the bed as Blaine left the room so she could freshen up.

Melody had asked Blaine to show her around the town to see all the beautiful sights once again as she knew she was getting to the end of her days. She wore the gown she wore on the day of the dance to remind her of the happy day she had staying with Blaine and his family.

Blaine didn't utter a word of what they wanted since she got back home until that morning. Melody also had been thinking of how that night will be as she had not been able to communicate with the white wolf. It was during her time of loneliness that she began to think of so many things that she had not thought of before.

She accepted the fact that she owed the sixteen years that she had lived after the cancer to the white wolf who had cured her cancer by staying in her, but she had always misused this opportunity of life as she merely allowed herself to exist during those years. She, like a lone wolf, deserted all humans and severed all forms of relationships that she could have had. Her mind went back to the time where her uncle told her of the sadness that gripped him as she was always acting cold towards everything and everyone. Instead of changing then, she became more withdrawn from everything except her music and the wolf.

She would have never realized her mistake if she hadn't came back to the town where it all started. She had always thought that love didn't exist, that it was mere folktales until she met this family and now all that she had denied herself was given to her in abundance which made her regret all the love that she had turned away.

She also looked at it from another end that all the happiness and comfort that she felt while with Blaine was meant to dissuade her from her mission. Even with that, with all the love and urge to stay with Blaine and to be loved to the end of her days, she never once had doubts about her goals.

It was time for her to let go of her companion and she knew she would miss the wolf as she could not imagine a life without it. She looked up as if talking to heaven.

"I passed your test. I didn't neglect my mission," she uttered as she rose up.

A cup of tea had been prepared for her downstairs, so with the blanket wrapped around her, she picked it and headed to the porch to enjoy the fresh air and feel the sun on her face. When the day was gradually moving to the evening, Blaine informed his aunt, cousin, and sister that he would like to spend some time with Melody alone so they would be camping away from home that evening. They all understood what he meant as he would love to make the most of the time they had left. Melody gave him a questioning look and this made him walk in her direction.

"I know what you are thinking." He announced as he sat beside her. "We have a few hours before nightfall, so I think it's best if we head out now. I have prepared enough food that will last us the journey." he informed her.

She had wanted to ask if he was going to bring a gun along but for some reason, she didn't. Blaine had a brilliant smile aimed at her just like the first day she saw him. But something was different with his smile this time. She didn't need the power of the wolf to know that the smile was a forced one, trying to shield her from the sadness that had overwhelmed him. She felt sorry for him, as she knew all that he was feeling as well all the other family members was her fault.

She stood up to get dressed and wore a gown that was similar to the one she used to wear in her trance to the oak tree. When she made it back downstairs, Blaine covered her body with his jacket as they headed out into his truck.

She didn't know the exact place the temple was but Ishtar had told her that she would be drawn to it anytime she was ready to go. She instructed Blaine to go the lake opposite the direction of the oak tree and park beside it where the vehicle won't be noticed.

They got there after about twenty minutes of rocky drive. And just a few feet from where he parked, they saw a small path that they can pass up to the hill. There was little they could see from up ahead as the mountain was always covered with fog. The fog was not a natural one as it was meant to shield the temple from prying eyes in order to keep its treasures and reverence secret as times were changing.

Blaine had carried a backpack that he slung over his shoulder, where he packed all that they would need for their journey to the Asher Temple. The journey to the temple was longer than they thought, and Blaine was happy that they had decided to start it long before the time they would need to be at the temple.

The moment they stepped into the woods that led up to the mountain, Melody felt the presence of wolves around them. But when she looked she didn't see anything, but her instincts were alerted of their presence even though she was not sure of the precise number. She remained alert for the time they would try to make a move against her, although a part of her was telling her that they were not going to. Blaine led the way guiding her through the hills and into the fog. They noticed that the higher they moved the heavier the fog became as they could not see what they had left behind.

BEHIND THE TREES AND FOG, KRIS AND RYAN WERE WATCHING OVER THE duo who were making the journey. Sage was the last to join them as she was sent to look around to see if she could scent or see Manofield and his new band of misfits.

Sage had gone farther than where they were and then back to town but it was as if Manofield had vanished into the thin air. During his search, she had the chance to reflect on their actions of the past and what they were presently doing. A feeling of anger surged in her when she remembered what Manofield was planning behind their back. He had made everybody believe that he was doing all that he was doing for the greater good of the pack and they were ready to do anything to make the plan work, even if it meant their death, as they saw it as a sacrifice that must be made for the greater good.

He didn't tell them all along the reason why he had wanted to kill the human family that Melody had grown attached to. He knew all along what the condition for splitting from the wolf would be and he knew that if he killed all those she loved; it won't be possible for her to be free of the white wolf.

"I was so stupid," she berated herself, not able to believe that she had fallen for the trick planned by him.

But after thinking about it for some time, she realized that it was inconceivable for her or any of the pack members would have known as they had been together for years now. She gave the assumedly good news to Ryan who was now serving as the leader of the pack but he didn't look joyous as she was. Sage was not sure why he still looked agitated and still on the edge of his toes.

"You don't seem pleased to hear that Manofield is not on to us," she commented.

Ryan looked at her then at Kris before talking.

"I am sorry for that, but regardless of where he is, he will show up to try to stop Melody from separating herself from the white wolf." he said before giving any further explanation. "You remember that he wants to marry her for the vast power that she has and it won't do him any good if she separated the wolf from her."

"Well, he can marry the wolf after," Kris teased and for a moment there, they laughed and almost forgot their pending issue.

"Eyes up," Ryan ordered again.

The three of them concentrated on the people they were guarding and they were surprised that Melody didn't act as if she was aware of their presence. Ryan shook his head in pity, as he knew that she must have been weakened to the extent that she was unable to tap into her werewolf part. It worked two ways for them as this would prevent her from attacking them if she thought that they were still enemies, and a wounded wolf can be exceptionally easy to kill while on the other hand, it would make her susceptible to attack as she would neither be able to defend herself or the human she so needed for the separation ritual to work. Anytime he thought of them losing, the vision of being blessed by Ishtar still lingered in his head and it kept motivating him into pressing on with his mission.

He looked at Kris and wondered how much he had grown and how badly he had treated him and yet, he joined him in the cause without looking back at the ways in which he was treated by him. Even with his young age, he respected the maturity and wisdom expressed by him. He knew in his heart that he would make a good Alpha one day-- if he made it out of the war alive.

Ryan gave a new order that they should flank Blaine and Melody just in case their enemies would attack from the other side. Sage and Kris maintained their position while Ryan moved gently to the other side of the road. He heaved a sigh of relief when he was not noticed by any of them. With this new arrangement, Sage was able to look at Melody for the first time since their attack on her human family.

She felt sorry for her, as she had grown very lean, even the big coat could not cover the emaciation that had occurred to her frame and for this Sage felt sorry for her. She felt guilty and because she knew if they had not attacked her in the first place, she would have carried on with her already burdensome journey without the addition of extra trouble and the strain they put on her system.

Melody missed a step and almost stumbled. Kris stood up to help and was quickly held back by Sage who reminded him that they could not afford to make their presence known until it was needed the most. She ruffled his hair to commend him for trying to help the poor lady.

Blaine was quick to keep her from falling. He knew she was already weary of the trekking. It had only been twenty minutes since they started walking with no hope of getting to the Temple any time soon. Melody looked at Blaine who was trying his best to not to let his sadness be obvious.

"We still have lots of time before we need to be there, how about we stop and get some rest?" Blaine offered.

Melody nodded in agreement and they sat on the stone that almost made her fall. Blaine brought out some water bottles from the bag and handed one over to her. When they had enough water, Melody called Blaine over to her and held on to his hand before speaking.

"Can I ask you a question Blaine and you will answer me honestly?" she inquired.

Blaine promised that he was going to answer her candidly, then she asked her question.

"Do you ever regret meeting me?" she asked, turning her eyes away from him as she could not stand the sadness that engulfed his face after asking the question.

She had been contemplating this question since they found out about her and no matter how much she felt she should not ask she wanted him to give her an answer instead of just assuming. Blaine took his hands away from Melody and stood up from beside her then he turned his back against her looking into the bush where Ryan was hiding.

"Melody, when I said you are the best thing to ever happen to me, I meant it," he told her then he sat beside her again now cuddling her.

Melody apologized for asking, as she was just feeling guilty for what she was making him have to go through and all that wouldn't have happened if they hadn't fallen in love with each other. Blaine looked at her, and then he spoke in a very clear voice.

"Love is not scheduled. Love is like a musical composition. It starts with a single note...then it eventually mates with a chorus to produce the most beautiful melody." he said with a grin.

Melody smiled at the analogy.

"Hmm. That is a good one," she commented with a smile.

"Well, you are not the only musician here," he teased as he winked at her cheekily.

In that brief moment it actually felt as if they were going for an actual camping trip, but as fast as the happiness came, it was swallowed by sadness. When they had enough rest, Blaine stood up and picked Melody up too. Their strength had been renewed with just a little rest and a bar of chocolate. Melody looked up then pointed upward.

"The temple of Asher is behind that hill," she said.

Just a few miles away, behind a tree with a very large root laid Manofield. His wound had gotten better. He had just been informed by one of his new pack members of Blaine and Melody's whereabouts, he smiled as he made himself more discreet.

"Come to me my love," he murmured as he made to intercept his bride. .

17

———

The sun was already setting. The once bright sun was already becoming orange, dull behind the clouds. Blaine and Melody got to the Asher Temple just in time for them to rest before they carried on with their mission.

The Asher Temple was not much of a temple now, it looked like a desolated house of the supernatural that had been left untended to for centuries. The temple was without a roof and the only demarcation that it was once a building was just the tall round pillars that stood all around what used to be the place of worship for the monks and holy men. The pillar was very tall and it was as if it extended to the sky.

Seeing the pillars, Melody remembered the pillars at the Manhattan Hall only those had a gargoyle attached to it, the pillars of the Asher Temple had skulls of different animals. She was sure that there might be the skull of werewolves or even humans emblazoned there too.

There were lots of markings on the pillars and they all looked the same when Melody examined three with her superior sight. She informed Blaine that the instruction on what they had to do when the comet comes had already been carved on the pillar. Melody had the feeling that it was one of the reasons why the temple was destroyed and even kept hidden with very heavy fog.

They set down beside a pillar that was very close to the altar, Blaine brought out a meal and drink for them to eat for them to be refreshed. Melody looked into the darkness to see if they had been followed but she didn't see or feel the presence of Manofield or any of the werewolves.

She noticed that since they stepped into the bush for the journey, her wolf sense had been back to the way it was before she fell sick ad she was happy for that as she knew that if everything worked out, it meant it will be the last she would be able to have those feelings.

She thought of how her life would be without hearing sounds made from a very long distance or even have the strength that she used to have. Blaine had packed some dry firewood so he used it to start a fire to keep them warm.

They sat beside each other quietly waiting for the comet and also praying that Manofield had a change of heart, which they knew, was impossible. As Melody ate the last chunk from her burger, Blaine began to talk.

"I must say this is surprising." he commented.

"What do you mean Blaine?" Melody asked not sure what he meant by his comment.

Blaine looked at her then chuckled, "I was born and raised in this town and yet I did not know that this temple even existed." he said.

"I guess I know more of this town than you thought then," Melody teased.

They both laughed softly at this as they continued their conversation.

"What exactly was this temple used for?" he asked feeling curious about the temple.

Melody didn't know much about the history; she only got to know about the temple and its location through her intuition or probably through the guidance of the wolf. And as she got the direction from inside her, she felt she knew the entire history behind the temple of Asher.

"It was said," she started telling Blaine the story. "That the temple of Asher belonged to a very powerful spiritual leader who reigned over humans and animals alike, as he was a werewolf like me. After much ruling and seeing that unlike him, his werewolf subjects could not exercise self-control like he could, he turned into a human by doing the exact thing that we want to do today. It was the power of the comet and love that made the splicing of the human from the wolf possible. History also has it that after the split, the wolf that left his body stayed to guard him against enemies who wanted to kill him for his power or out of jealousy. One day as fate would have it, he was killed by a dangerous man from the neighboring clan. Since that time, the wolf swore to avenge its master, as he was innocent loving and kind and did not deserve to meet his death that way. After years of hunting, the wolf was able to avenge its master, but what didn't happen after the death of his master's murderer was the feeling of peace he expected to find. The wolf could never bring itself out of the pain of losing its master even after a long time, so it killed himself." Melody paused in order to allow him to digest the first part of the story before moving to the major part.

"The mother wolf having seen the kind of love that the wolf had for its master didn't receive it into the Wolverdome, the wolf's paradise and instead, she allowed the wolf to be reborn as the white wolf. That is the history of the first white wolf, how the species came into existence. Although, centuries later they were hunted out of greed and envy as they were the purest of all breeds. During that time, the Asher Temple was revisited by the white wolves as their abode and fortress. Being a special species, the white wolf was not bound by the curse of the full moon, so it could transform as it pleased. The white wolf is a symbol of purity and peace," Melody said as she finished narrating the story she had no knowledge of just a few minutes ago.

Blaine was silent for a while as he played with Melody's fingers, Melody looked at him and smiled. Blaine having heard the story understood why the white wolf decided to stay with Melody all these years. Melody, like the white wolf, was a pure person.

"I fell in love with the purest of all hearts," he thought to himself. "My very own heart song."

As they enjoyed the warmth of each other's arms Melody broke away suddenly from him. She had heard something heading their way. It was the sound of footsteps made by two or three people. She was not sure about the exact number, but what she was sure of was they were coming their way. Fast.

Blaine wanted to ask what was wrong when she suddenly stood up, but just as he was about to ask, his gaze traveled to where Melody was looking at and suddenly, three humans jumped out of the forest gasping for air as they moved closer to them. It was Kris, Sage, and Ryan. Melody moved towards them as she made a gesture to Blaine to stay where he was.

Blaine, on the other hand, had come with a Desert Eagle pistol knowing that mere human strength could not overcome their ruthless and beastly creatures. He reached for it from where he kept it tucked away from Melody's sight, waiting for the right time to use it.

Melody on the other hand, knew that the three werewolves in front of her were her enemies had a feeling that they were not there to attack them. She connected the dots that they were the presence that she felt when they entered the forest and if they wanted to kill them, they would have done that easily on the way and it didn't make sense for them to wait till this crucial moment to act.

"What are you guys doing here?" Melody asked making sure her voice was stern and yet not disrespectful. She was not sure of their mission, so she wanted to tread carefully.

"We're here to protect you," Kris replied beating the others to it.

"We are here to make sure that whatever you want to do is successful. We really are sorry for everything that we have done to you, Manofield manipulated us all," Ryan said building off of what Kris had hurriedly said.

Blaine was relieved to hear this, as fighting them off was the last thing on his mind.

Ryan wanted to fill them in on what was going to happen but he had no sooner started talking, that they heard another set of footsteps running fiercely towards them. There was no mistaking the way they were running.

"It's like they are coming from all around us," Melody commented.

Ryan laughed at this then explained to her that they were just six including their master Manofield, and the reason why it sounded that way was because of the diversionary tactic he was using, he called it the Encompassing Wolf Guerilla Tactic, where small forces were made to sound very large in order to kill the fighting spirit of their enemies.

They looked up at the same time and they saw that the first comet was upon them even though it was yet to be visible to the naked eye. They knew without a doubt that it was time.

"We will hold them off," Sage told them quickly. "But you have about ten minutes to do whatever thing you want to do majestic white wolf," she said.

Melody gave her a nod while she bowed gently in respect to her. Ryan, Kris, and Sage moved back from them and they immediately shifted into their wolf forms. Ryan was looking very large, larger than before. His body was already recognizing the new leadership position that he was in. Unbeknownst to him, he had automatically become an alpha, as his eyes had already turned from yellow to red and black because of the power he drew from Kris and Sage.

They bowed one more time to Melody, who wished them best of luck before they entered the forest again from different angles. Blaine was dumbstruck in seeing this as it was his first time to see a transformation up close and was amazed that Melody was not moved by any of this.

When they were out of sight, the duo went back into the temple, instead of staying where their bags were, Melody took Blaine to the altar used by the first person to split from his werewolf side centuries ago.

The altar was made of fine mud and it was enveloped by gold that had been melted in a way that it now served as a chain in holding together the animal skin used in wrapping it together. Blaine embraced Melody and they kissed each other for quite some time before setting to work.

Blaine brought out the knife and handed it over to Melody. She pressed the tip of the knife to her palm till blood started seeping out. She clenched her fist tightly in pain, as she handed the knife back to Blaine for him to do the same. Melody stretched her bloody hand towards Blaine who held her hand with his too. Having combined their blood, they both looked up to the sky. The comet was now visible to all that were on earth. It was a ball of fury, hot stone with the tail of fire falling fast across the surface of the earth making the light from the full moon irrelevant. They looked at each other and smiled, having seen the beautiful sight in the sky. As the comet was getting closer to earth, the pain from their palms became excruciating. The blood had not stopped dripping from their hands but regardless; they did not let go of their hands.

Blaine didn't take his gaze off Melody as his mind kept reminding him of her selfless attitude towards the wolf. Melody could feel the warmth of the falling comet. She closed her eyes as she whispered to herself knowing that the comet would pass over the two of them by the stroke of midnight.

"You will be free soon, my love."

18

———————

The comet was blazing across the night sky now. As the light from the comet shone over the hill, it illuminated the temple of Asher. Blaine and Melody according to the hieroglyphs on the pillars had passed the first stage, which was presenting the blood of the lover so it would be known that the person is ready to make any form of sacrifice to their counterpart.

They let go of each other's hand but they were still facing each other. So far, there had not been any trouble for them, Blaine was silently thankful that the three werewolves that were terrorizing them were not with them. He imagined how it would have turned out if it were just him and Melody. Blaine looked down to the ground and as he looked at Melody from her feet, he noticed something on her right leg.

She had a bite mark and the mark was bleeding profusely. She staggered to the back as the loss of blood began to weaken her then, she drifted to the floor gradually. She blinked slowly as she tried to remain conscious till the sacrifice was done. She closed her eyes for the second time, but when she did her best to open them again, she found herself in the woods close to the cabin she was kept in when she was just five years old. She had found herself in the past, the very day that the white wolf cured her and the bite mark on her leg was identical to the one made by the wolf years ago. It all was coming back to her in waves of pain, and it was as if the bite was just made by the white wolf, but it was her past that was haunting her as it had been since she was cured.

Blaine had rushed to her to get a hold of her but he stopped short when he saw another threat. From the shadows made by one of the pillars in the temple emerged a large brown wolf with part of his fur having a grey color. His eyes were red like a burning coal used in powering the engine of the ancient train. It moved tautly towards them but had his eyes fixed on Blaine. Without much thought, Blaine knew it was the alpha that he shot a few days ago. He wondered how fast he had healed from his bullet wound and there was clearly no scar to show for his shot.

The wolf kept moving in a roundabout way towards Blaine. Melody felt the presence of Manofield and she knew that Blaine might not be able to take on the alpha. With her pain shifting it was going to be difficult but she had to at least try, she bent to morph into the white wolf but no matter how hard she tried, she was unable to get a hold of her animal self. The intense pain that was wracking her body was the main cause for this, as shifting required a high degree of concentration to get hold of the other side. She was already at a crucial moment that would define how the splitting would go. If she was successful in shifting to the white wolf she would be at risk of remaining a wolf all her life, and yet she could not bring herself to allow Blaine to lose his life because of her.

She looked up but her sight was already blurry, only her other wolf senses were still there although they were already waning. Luckily for the two of them, Ryan in his wolf form came out of the bush where he had been hidden all along.

With the element of surprise, he attacked Manofield from his side and hurled him with all his might against one of the pillars in the temple. The force he used was so great that it made the pillar fall. Again, Melody tried to shift, as she didn't like the fact that she was not doing anything to help when everyone was fighting and risking their lives on her behalf. The harder she tried to become a wolf, the more severe, and agonizing the pain became for her.

Ryan had tactically drawn the battle away from where Melody was. When Blaine looked at them from the distance, he knew that Ryan did not have the upper hand in the fight. This caused him to worry about Melody's life, as he knew that the moment Ryan was defeated, Manofield would in all his anger and blood thirst rip him into pieces.

He began to think of the ways in which he might be able to help Melody, he thought of the gun but knew it would not do anything to save them as a even a bigger gun could not stop Manofield the other day, so the possibility of a pistol doing any damage was very slim. Blaine knelt beside Melody to see how she was faring. Tears were already flowing from their eyes and only one idea came to Blaine's mind on how to save Melody.

Although it was not the best of ideas, it was the only thing he could think of that would not only save Melody but also the others. When he told Melody of it, she wept harder and forbade him from doing it.

"Melody, look at me," he said holding her head with his hands. "You have got to bite me now. You cannot turn now because of the pain, I am the only one to carry the burden. I am willing to do this for you... for us. If this is my last moment as human, I will gladly accept my fate and save you." he said.

Melody nodded in affirmation having been convinced by him.

"To live for love is to die for love," he said "To make a song, sometimes you need a chorus. I will not let it end this way. I will not let you end this way."

Now taking one of his hands to her mouth he shouted but the tears drowned it, "Do it," he ordered.

Melody had thought of it too, she knew what Blaine asked would not only change him but also everything for his family and yet he was willing to take the risk. She had wondered for a short period of time if being a werewolf was a curse or a blessing. It was the question that she had always asked herself since the day she killed her parents.

As she prepared to turn Blaine, Ryan's body was flung close to where the altar was. He had sustained a fatal blow on his neck and was bleeding uncontrollably. His strength could not hold on to his wolf form, so he morphed back to his human form. He knew he was the last line of defense for the two of them, as Sage and Kris had other missions to attend to. He also knew that, if Melody and Blaine died, everything they had done would be for nothing.

With all hope all boiled down to one last shot, Melody closed her eyes to make a wish, and then it was granted. She was still in her human form but her teeth had turned to that of the majestic white wolf. Biting swiftly down, she bit Blaine in his arm.

Blaine drew away from her in pain as the venom of the wolf traveled faster than he would have thought. He could feel it moving all over his body through his bloodstream. He felt cold as if he was dying then all of a sudden he became stiff like a corpse.

Melody looked at him and she screamed in anguish at what she had done. Her scream pierced Blaine's ears and he jumped up in pain. As he opened his eyes, his blue eyes were replaced with yellow-grey color. He shouted in pain because of his bones making the transformation. The sounds of his bones restructuring could be heard by Melody and she knew what was going on- he was making his first transformation into a werewolf, and not just any werewolf but the majestic white wolf.

The transformation took longer than Melody's typically did while lots of blood filled the floor. His clothes were no more and his once handsome well-chiseled face was replaced with a gigantic long snout, which suited his large white furry body.

He rose to his feet when the transformation was complete and he was no longer Blaine but a white wolf. He turned around to comprehend where he was, but he noticed that he could still feel a connection to his human self and it was just the case of the wolf being in the driver's seat.

Blaine gave a loud howl to the sky facing the comet. He heard the growl from behind him. When he turned, he saw the big brown wolf barring his teeth as a threat to him. His mouth was dripping with blood which was certainly from Ryan's wound. Blaine glanced over at Melody and she was barely moving. He felt for her as she was on the brink of losing her life. When Blaine and Manofield's eyes locked, it was as if Manofield was smiling at him then it suddenly turned into a broad frown. He was vexed that Blaine had just taken what he now referred to as his reason for existence but before he could think things through, the new white wolf charged against him biting and crawling all over his body. They rolled on the floor in agony till they fell downhill into the forest.

When it was all quiet again at the altar, Melody struggled to look around and didn't see anybody. She was already bleeding from the wounds she had sustained. Her fast healing ability was no longer with her and she could not feel her tissues repairing like they used to.

Blood was also trickling out of her mouth and it made her choke. Her tears had run dry by that time, she was tired, tired of everything that was happening, and all she wanted was for everything to end. Her mind started picking random memories, she remembered the taste of her parents' blood in her mouth, the day she finally learned how to control the beast side of her. She thought of how loving her uncle was, even though she remained cold and withdrawn from him and from others that had tried to come close to her. She did not only think of the undone part of her years but also the times she did the best things, the things that made her heart sing. .

Marina's smile and her warm hugs came to her memory, the time Sandy and her went to town and talked about guys, the time Zane tried getting a date for her with Blaine, her first kiss with him, everything kept coming to her in a flash like a movie projector.

"Could this be it?" she thought to herself.

She had always thought of how death would be and had made quite a number of speculations but she never thought that it would be like this. Her entire life rushed to her mind at once and she was able to comprehend it. All of a sudden she heard a voice. It was first strange to her, then after a while she felt she knew the voice, she had heard it before. Then another voice, a male one this time spoke again.

She might be having second thoughts on whose voice the first female speaker could be, but the second was very clear to her and for the past sixteen years, she kept the voices in her memory. From the darkness, she saw her parents smiling at her.

"You are a survivor, my dear Sophia." David; her father said.

"But it is time to stop fighting. Come home love, come to us." Her mother Candace added and they disappeared as fast as they came.

Melody smiled and gradually her breathing began to stop.

19

———————

The grass in which Blaine and Manofield had rolled in was already painted with blood from the both of them. They had fought fiercely with the two of them sustaining fatal wounds. As one bit, the other scratched and yet none of them gave out a noise of pain. They had made a silent vow to settle things amongst themselves without aid from anybody.

Further down the hill, Kris and Sage were also bathed in blood but only some of it was from themselves, most of the blood on their bodies were of the new pack members. Although Manofield had picked them from the most unholy places, and without the strength of the werewolf would have succumbed to the battle. But being inexperienced with the way the beast worked, they were unable to have a better angle of the fight which made them suffer lots of wounds from the more experienced Sage and Kris.

While fighting them they had intentionally drew them far away from their alpha, which would make it very hard for them to howl for help and if they did, it won't be easy for Manofield to come to their rescue. When most of his pack had already been slaughtered, one of them managed to escape; it first tried to run for his life but having a sense of loyalty, he raced to give a helping hand to its leader.

He could see that the fight between him and the white wolf was very bloody and tight, so it quietly hid itself behind the bush, waiting for just the right time to attack. Blaine had biffed Manofield with his paws and this made him stagger backward in pain. Seeing that Blaine was clear, the wolf sideswiped him making Blaine disoriented, as he didn't know from where the attack had come precisely. Seeing that Blaine was no longer focused on the battle with him, Manofield took the opportunity to strike a lasting blow on him. He jumped through the air with his teeth bared and his claws pointed forward as he landed on Blaine's back. Instinctively, Blaine tried to get him off his back but his claws were already planted deep in his muscles, which made him yelp in pain.

Manofield was furious knowing that a filthy human had stolen all that he wanted. Because of this, he had made up his mind that he was going to make him pay and regret ever taking the power of the white wolf and all the knowledge that it had. Blaine was able to push him off his back and he also landed a deep cut with his claws to his face before he could move further away.

The pack member that had helped Manofield the other time rushed towards Blaine, but Blaine was not planning on making the same mistake twice. So when he moved fast against him, he drifted to the right causing him to miss his target. Before he could turn towards Blaine, he felt sharp teeth cut into his flesh and his blood started flowing. He squealed in pain as he also tried to get a hold of its attacker but he couldn't.

With its mouth the white wolf threw it towards Manofield. By this time, the comet was about to touch down somewhere far away and Blaine knew it was over and the only thing they all needed was to win this battle, it was the only way they could get out of there alive. Manofield was enraged at the way his pack member had been battered, he wanted to rip the life out of Blaine but no matter how hard he tried, he could not as the power of the white wolf was immense. He charged against Blaine again, this time determined to overpower him. But as he moved closer to him, a strange figure attacked him from the side.

He didn't see who the wolf was but it had grabbed his neck tight and it took all his effort to break free, which only proved to cause him more injury and pain. The wolf snapped his neck making his blood vessels break away. Manofield felt weakened and used up and then he saw that his doom was unavoidable. Light flashed to his face then everything was dark. He thought for a while if that was going to be the end of him- the great Manofield. He could picture Ishtar seeing him and making fun of him like he did the day he went to him. Almost resigning to his fate, he tried to look at his killer and having seen that Manofield was now too weak to launch any deadly attack against anyone, his neck was released.

As Manofield turned, he couldn't believe his eyes. His first thought was that the attacker was one of his initial pack members who had betrayed him, but what was in front of him was not something he would have ever thought of. He looked at Blaine and then at the wolf in front of him.

He had been attacked by another majestic white wolf, who was just slightly smaller in stature than Blaine. He fell to the ground and began to crawl towards where the altar was to get a logical explanation to what was happening. He had just moved a few feet away from where he started when his strength could no longer hold him as an alpha wolf, so he transformed back to his human form. His face was covered in blood and likewise his shirt. His legs had been bitten and his arms had also sustained considerable wounds too. But none of these things mattered to him at the moment, he had to see what had happened in the altar for himself.

On reaching the alter, what he saw left him as curious as ever. Blaine had stopped attacking him and instead followed him gently to the altar as he was also surprised to see the white wolf who assisted in launching a counter attack. On the altar was Melody, she was lifeless on the alter bathed in her own blood and Ryan also laid at the foot of the altar. Before they died, Ryan had helped Melody up to the altar while he fell to the ground just beside it.

Sage and Kris also met them there. On seeing the scene, they both transformed back to their human forms. Sage ran to where Ryan laid. She started beating him and slapping his face as she shouted his name. Tears began to stream out of her eyes and Kris knelt feeling dejected as he also wept. Blaine had also turned back to his human form now and was beside Melody.

He didn't care the amount of blood around her; he hugged her as he wept silently. There was no hope for her as she was cold and lifeless. He let out a loud shout having noticed that she was gone away from him forever. Her blood stained his clothes and when he looked in the direction that Manofield was before, he was gone.

It no longer mattered to him as the love of his life, the reason he took this burdensome journey was dead. They were still mourning their death when a white wolf came out of the bush. Blaine had almost forgotten about the white wolf and he wondered who it might be. She moved closer to where Ryan laid and sniffed him out. It then moved back as it began to morph.

Light shone all around the wolf as it shifted and this made it impossible for any of them to see who it was. But as the light died down, they all could not believe who the white wolf was. It was Melody. Blaine looked at the body he was holding and before his eyes, it turned to dust and it was washed away by the gust of wind. Blaine stood up as he moved closer to Melody. His first thought was that she was a ghost, but that would be impossible as she didn't disappear or use any ghostly means to attack Manofield.

"Ryan is alive," Melody spoke quietly.

It was really her. Her voice was exactly like the first time he heard it except that it was not full of life. Kris helped Sage in picking up Ryan from his own blood and he also attest to the fact that he was still alive although barely.

"But...How?" Blaine stuttered.

"Yes I know, my dear Blaine," she said. "I am Wolf Song...and I am Also Melody Sophia. You see, when I was bitten as a child I held onto my humanity and never really allowed the wolf to entirely take over to become one with my soul. I had subjected it to a prison, which it didn't complain of, and this was the reason my cancer came back. I have made myself more human than wolf as opposed to striking a balance. When I was dying, it was then that I understood the main purpose of this ritual. It allowed my wolf side to separate from my human side but it did not separate me from who I am destined to be. Who we are destined to be the wolf and myself. I am still the same girl you fell in love with. My wolf name is Wolf Song and my human name still remains Melody Sophia" she explained.

It was as if Blaine's whole world just took an unexpected but good turn and he was very happy, he moved close to her now and reached out and touched her hand. They felt each other's essence with this and then Blaine was certain that it was Melody.

Not too far from where they stood, Manofield had tried to escape but he stopped short not able to carry himself any further. He fell to the ground and his sight became blurry as his breathing became harder and more labored. Then with ease, he gave his last breath.

EPILOGUE

The sky above was clear as the weather was conducive for birds and animals of different forms who could be seen playing around. The butterfly could be seen sucking the nectar of flowers. It was like they were in paradise with all the perfection that nature had brought to them.

Voices of people could be heard outside the house. They were chattering about different things which all made them laugh at almost anything said by their counterpart. Sage's bruises had healed, as her face was looking fresh and vibrant. She was standing in front of the Chorus house right next to Sandy and Marina.

They had the same type of dress on; a purple gown that was embellished with feathers and flowers from the forest. The three of them were happy when they were told by Melody that she would be needing them to be her bridesmaids. Although Sage didn't think herself worthy of such consideration because of all that she had done, she was persuaded by Melody who told her that they were going to be friends forever.

Zane and Kris were looking dashing in their blue suits with their hair well combed. When they went out to meet the ladies, they were being taunted as the ladies could barely recognize them.

"It will be better to get yourself someone here with your outfit or you will have to forget about it," Marina told Zane jokingly.

"Well, maybe we can be lucky like Blaine," Kris answered.

They all laughed at this as Marina gave them a hug before they moved away. They went back to the house to see how Blaine was faring with his outfit, but they were surprised to see that he was just standing by the mirror half naked.

"What in the world is going on?" Kris exclaimed seeing that he had yet to get dressed.

"I sure hope that is not how you plan on appearing to your wedding," Zane teased him.

"Well, I still look strikingly handsome regardless," he replied smiling at him.

Although he was trying to cover up his nervousness, it was very obvious. Zane and Kris tried to encourage him and after much talk, he felt better. He wore a tuxedo that he had picked himself from the boutique. It had a strong resemblance to the one he wore in the dream he had in the cave. He took a deep breath before telling Kris to open up the door for him.

The orchestra was already playing softly, entertaining the guests that had graced his wedding with their presence. He started moving to the front, greeting everyone as he passed. On getting to the altar, which was raised higher than the ground where everybody stood, he turned towards them.

"This is it," is muttered to himself.

The song the orchestra was playing changed to welcome the presence of the bride. She was wearing a white gown that had a touch of silver all over it. She was being escorted by Ryan as she walked down the aisle towards him. Even with the veil, Blaine could see her gorgeous face and the charming smile that had lightened the burden in his life.

As they got to the front, she could perceive the happiness and joy in Marina's heart. Marina had been elated since they got back from 'camping' only to discover that Melody had been cured of the cancer. She went the extra mile in making sure the diagnoses were right but having tried lots of doctors, they all arrived at the same conclusion- Melody had been miraculously cured of cancer and she was healthier than ever before.

Melody Sophia was not just herself again, she was better, she had taken up and accepted her wolf name Wolf Song and her destiny with Blaine Chorus who turned out to be the missing piece in her life.

She had not only found love but had also provided a worthy counterpart for the white wolf making it have a companion in whom they can protect the town. The procession and ceremony happened so fast and during that period, Blaine didn't take his gaze off her. He was so happy that his wish had come to pass and he had also helped Melody fulfill her wish- to save the white wolf.

They turned towards the crowd after their first kiss as man and wife, and were surprised to see Ishtar being part of the audience. The other werewolves present knew the look and they gazed towards where they were looking. They smiled on seeing Ishtar who made a sign of cheers with a glass of wine. He was not seen by any of the other people present and like a gust of wind, the couple could hear him bless and wish them all the best in their newly forged family and responsibility.

They didn't understand the responsibility part so decided to ask him when the ceremony is over. But Ishtar had other plans. He had been in existence since the first comet where the splitting occurred and had been the protector of the forest and town even before they had a name. But now, he felt his mission had been accomplished. He knew the town would be in safe hands with Blaine Chorus and Wolf Song guarding it.

"My work here is done," he whispered but it seemed all the were-wolves heard him and upon hearing the pronouncement as husband and wife, he gave a broad smile and like the air from his nose, and then he disappeared leaving behind an envelope where he sat.

The celebration extended to late in the evening and it didn't seem as if it would come to an end anytime soon as people were still saying their congratulations.

"I didn't know you had lots of people as friends," Melody commented jokingly.

"Well, I can say the same thing about you," he replied as he turned his gaze to Melody's maestro and friends from the orchestra. She didn't know they were around until that time and was very happy to see them. They apologized for coming so late as they had a recital that day too. One of them decided to play the famous notes of Melody and what once caused her to cry and brought joy to her heart.

After another long hour of celebration, Blaine was getting tired.

"Can we sneak off now?" he asked Melody with a wink.

"Wait, you want us to leave everybody here and sneak away to our house?" she asked looking at him as if he were crazy.

"Yes," Blaine answered not sure what Melody thought about that.

"Count me in," she said laughing hysterically.

The left the party without being noticed by most people but the werewolves felt their presence depart from them. They had already built a cabin close to the oak tree. It would allow them to communicate with the wolves inside them and also act like the guardians of the forest that they were. The room had pictures of their lives hung on the wall. Sandy had done more than that by putting all the pictures of them she took without them knowing in a frame using them as a decoration around the house. They sat on the bed tired and in silence they thought about how happy their life had turned out and how beautiful and joyful their new life would be together.

ABOUT THE AUTHOR

'A dream is a glimpse of what you can have if you decide to walk down that path with no regrets...'

Alex H. Singh was born and raised in Toronto, Ontario. He is single and still lives in the city today, with his cat, Karma, who is a Calico/Tortie mix.

He spent 3 years in University (UFT) and took a variety of courses, including English Literature and English Media. He decided, however, that a career on another path would be best for him and took a position as a Financial Advisor for a well-known and dependable bank, where he has worked ever since.

But it was to writing that Alex has always been drawn, and he has been penning books in various genres since he was 18. He has since self-published 13 books and particularly enjoys horrors, thrillers, sci-fi & Fantasy. He is keen to see what his growing army of fans will think of his *Fallen Kingdoms Chronicles Series*, *The Second Husband* and *Tapestry Series* which are all set for release.

In his spare time, Alex is a big fan of taking short naps as it helps to rejuvenate him. He also exercises regularly and enjoys baking, making old favorites like cupcakes, cheesecakes and other sweet treats. As a self-confessed foodie, he enjoys trying out new and delicious foods with friends, from a variety of eateries around the City.

Alex's hopes for the future are to keep on writing books that people will enjoy reading and perhaps one day be able to do it full-time. He has already attained bestseller lists on a popular digital platform but would love to reach the Holy Grail of making the NYT List one day.

You can contact or follow Alex H. Singh, or simply see what he is writing next.